THE WANDERER

DAHLIA DONOVAN

The Wanderer © 2017 by Dahlia Donovan

The Wanderer is a work of fiction. All names, characters, events and places found therein are either from the author's imagination or used fictitiously. Any similarity to persons alive or dead, actual events, locations, or organizations is entirely coincidental and not intended by the author.

For information, contact the publisher, Hot Tree Publishing.

WWW.HOTTREEPUBLISHING.COM

Editing: Hot Tree Editing

Formatting; RMGraphX

Cover Designer: Claire Smith

ISBN-10: 1-925448-76-2

ISBN-13: 978-1-925448-76-4

10 9 8 7 6 5 4 3 2 1

DEDICATION

To all the wanderers in my life—may you never truly be lost.

PROLOGUE

GRAHAM

Weddings.

Weddings were a pain more excruciating than a broken nose, or tooth, or both—an event to be avoided when at all possible. Only the blissfully ignorant would voluntarily submit themselves to the farce of "marital bliss," never mind the noise, whimpering women, and a priest who would undoubtedly drone on and on unless someone whacked him upside the head.

Why did I agree to this shit? If this bint sobs into my sleeve one more sodding time, I'll shove her into the aisle, manners be damned. I should've claimed a sudden bout of dengue fever in Macau and been done with it.

Graham Hodson had returned home early from yet another adventure to attend the wedding of his best mate,

Francis, and his soon-to-be husband, former rugby star Caddock Stanford. He'd contemplated doing a runner. His twin brother, Rupert, had threatened to drag him in by the ear, pointing out that they couldn't disappoint their childhood friend, could they?

Even if he were tempted to do so, Joanne, Rupert's wife, had promised untold pain if he did anything to ruin Francis's day. The spoilsport also vetoed all of his ideas to improve the day for the two grooms. He didn't see why they wouldn't enjoy having massive cod strung up to their escape vehicle.

Graham glanced across the room, and his mood brightened when he spotted an old mate, Jack Sasaki. They'd spent summers playing on Cornwall beaches together as kids, along with Rupert. They often flirted with the same boys, though one date with each other had been enough to realise they made far better friends.

The half-Japanese and half-Cornish man made his living as a barber a few villages over, in Fowey. Graham hadn't seen him in a while and would have to find time while home to have a beer and chat with him. He hoped Jack was having better luck romantically than he currently was.

Wanderlust didn't come with the perks of being romantically available. His passport might've been filled with stamps, but his nights had been filled with loneliness—aside from occasional casual sex. His adventures brought joy to his life.

I don't sodding need anyone to be happy.

Now, repeat the mantra until the wedding stops making

you act stupidly moody.

It might be the wedding of a close friend, but boredom continued to make his mind drift. Did anyone other than the couple care about the cute dog with a bow tie or the adorable child in the tuxedo? No. The answer would *always* be no. People went to ceremonies for the food and drink that followed after, and no one would ever be able to convince him otherwise.

A sniffle from the woman beside him was a reminder that maybe some people did care. With a less cynical view, Graham could admit the tuxedos had been well chosen. Tastefully done bouquets of white roses were adorned with pale blue ribbons that had antiqued copper rugby charms dangling from them.

Adorable.

Graham could also admit, however painfully, that the blissful happiness on Francis's face made him slightly envious. "Sodding weddings."

A gasp from the weepy twit reminded him not to mutter out loud. He summoned a smile when Francis glanced his way. The things one did for friends.

Oh, hello.

Who the bloody hell are you?

Never mind who you are. Can I see you naked?

An absolutely gorgeous bloke sitting on Caddock's side of the church had caught his attention. Tall, with a closely shaved head and black beard, he had a strong jaw—sharp lines all over really, from what Graham could see. He wore a suit that bordered on obscene for the way it clung to his muscled form.

Suddenly this event looks far more interesting than it did a minute ago. Now how do I get myself an introduction? Should be easy. It's a wedding; single people come to hook up at them, right?

Right.

Their eyes met. Almost identical grins of acknowledgement followed, which intrigued Graham. People didn't always read him so well. Mr Tall, Bald, and Gorgeous smirked as if he knew exactly what Graham had been thinking.

They'd *definitely* made a connection.

Interesting.

If the wedding ceremony hadn't been in full swing, Graham would've immediately wandered over to introduce himself. They settled for not so subtle flirtatious smirks. His impatience grew more palpable waiting for it to be over.

Their eyes continually drifted towards one another. An electric shock hit him each time. It sounded dramatic even in his head—but he did feel a mysterious sense of adventure just from contemplating a brief encounter with the mystery man.

The ceremony had barely ended, and the church cleared out before Graham found himself being crowded into an out of the way closet with the man. Their elbows bumped into shelves. His unnamed partner shushed him with a muffled snicker.

"Don't muck the suit up," Graham whispered when a strong hand gripped him firmly through his trousers and squeezed. He'd already been half-hard imagining what lay beneath the man's clothing. "Oh, bugger the suit, keeping doing that."

"Shut up."

A lovely rough voice to go with those hard fingers.

With the thrill of potentially being caught swirling around them like electricity in the air, Graham didn't have a chance for anything else. They fumbled around the cramped space while carefully trying to avoid knocking anything over. In the end, he had to practically bite through his lip to keep from crying out when they spent their orgasms into each other's hands.

Sharing names and numbers didn't even cross his mind. Why would it? It hadn't even been intercourse. They'd kissed, enjoyed the dexterity of each other's fingers—deftly slipping into trousers and pants without undressing—and managed to leave before anyone stumbled on their hiding place.

A quick wash of the hands, a straightening of my clothes and hair, and no one will ever be the wiser.

Rupert caught him skulking out of the church a few moments later. "What've you done now? Or should I say who? For fuck's sake, it's a wedding—and it's barely finished. How have you already gotten into someone's trousers?"

"Talent." He coughed through a burp, patting himself on the chest. *Sodding indigestion.* He'd been suffering with it for months. "Pure, raw talent."

"Well? Who was it?" His twin glanced around, trying to pick out the likely candidate. "Did you even get a name?"

Graham straightened his shirt and ran fingers through his reddish-blond hair to un-muss it. He gave his brother a grin. "Not a clue, not a Scooby-Doo."

"Oh, honestly." Rupert snorted loudly. "Are you ever

going to grow out of this shagging anyone on two legs?"

"I won't shag just anyone."

"Almost anyone."

"I shagged one—*one* of the people in this room." Graham refused to allow his eyes to search for the impressively built man he'd recently canoodled with in a church closet. "And we didn't actually shag."

"Close enough." Rupert shook his head at him. "Did you exchange anything useful? Names? Numbers?"

"Don't ask questions you don't want the answers to, Rup-Rup." Graham smirked at the choked response from his brother to the familiar nickname. "Go ask Joanne to dance with you. I'm going to see if there's any decent food—only good thing about attending this bloody event."

"Not the shagging?"

"We *didn't* shag." Graham shoved his brother in the direction of his wife. "*Arse.*"

It meant nothing.

So why am I sensing him from across the room?

Why can I still taste him?

CHAPTER ONE

GRAHAM
SIX MONTHS LATER...

When Graham found the plonker who had decided mid-January would be a brilliant time to visit Western Australia, the bastard would be taking a flying leap into a volcano. The stifling heat threatened to make him barmy. Forty sodding degrees Celsius. Forty. His brain was going to melt into a pile of goo, along with his camera.

Forty. Bloody. Degrees.

Maybe if I repeat the number a few more times, it won't feel as if I'm losing the will to live.

Hell, apparently, had no fury like a magazine editor scorned. Blowing off his deadline for picking a new destination had been a terrible idea. He would definitely select his own locations from now on to avoid death from heat stroke.

Good news? Graham could cook his bacon and eggs on a rock outside. Bad news? His tongue might have dried up to the point of sticking to the roof of his mouth. Maybe another beer—or thirty; things always looked up when getting sloshed was a possibility.

Was it too early to indulge? He glanced away from the hotel window towards the small fridge in the corner of the room. A morning beer couldn't hurt anything, could it?

One more day of photographs. One solitary, miserable twenty-four hours in the blinding heat before the blessed misty, foggy, cold shores of Cornwall called him home. He'd never thought the idea of gloomy winter months would bring such giddy joy to him.

His guide who accompanied him to all things local had provided him with a steady diet of TimTams and Tooheys. No wonder his gut had been in turmoil the whole trip. It had to be the crap diet. He rubbed absently at the tattoo on his right wrist—a chess knight saying "ni"—considering his options.

I hope it's the shit diet.

He closed his eyes against the bright sun shining through the window of his rented room in Cervantes, and found images of dark, laughing eyes going through his mind. The trip to Australia and the one to Singapore before it hadn't only been about fulfilling work commitments. He'd been running like a terrified schoolboy.

Bugger it all.

The anonymous pleasure he'd experienced at the wedding had become not so mysterious several months later. His cheeks still flushed uncharacteristically when recalling being *introduced* to Boyce Brooks. Rupert had been helping the former English international rugby star sort out a newly inherited property near Whitsand Bay Beach in Torpoint.

Boyce, or BC as he apparently preferred to be called, had been overly interested in the introduction, having pushed Rupert for it. Graham, on the other hand, had grabbed the first available assignment that let him get far away from anything that might even resemble a date. The knowing look on his twin's face had also encouraged the fleeing.

His twin could *always* be counted on to make a situation worse. Whatever BC had said to him, Rupert had obviously figured out he was the person Graham had wanked in the closet. The shrewd look told him his brother would be insufferable for months.

It was stupid. He *was* stupid. All of it was stupid—stupidity clearly ran amok.

The strong introductory handshake had been the only thing Graham could remember from his second encounter with the man, he'd been so completely thrown by it. No one had ever put him so off his game.

Stammering nervously didn't happen in his world when chatting up a hot bloke—or bird—and so Graham had fallen back on a tried and true method of getting himself out of awkward moments: he'd begun to quote Monty Python. It had always been an assured method of causing a laugh or two.

BC, it turned out, happened to be a *massive* fan. He'd lifted his shirt to reveal the rock-hard abs that Graham had felt, but not seen in the dark. The unveiling had also shown the chess piece tattoo on his side.

The same one Graham had on his wrist. They had the *same* tattoo—the same obsessive love of Monty Python. It had made him wonder what else they had in common.

Run. Running. Ran.

Cowardly ginger.

Ignoring the derision of his own thoughts, Graham checked his itinerary for the day. One visit to the nearby national park, along with photos later in the evening would be sufficient for his write-up on Western Australia. He hoped.

His next travel series would be centred on Cornwall. The London-based periodical wanted to highlight places closer to home for the rest of the year. They'd been confused when he'd initially tried to fob it off on someone else.

His editor had adamantly refused, and Graham's time in Hades—Australia—had changed his mind about it. He could suffer the potential humiliation from his twin and his one-hour stand if it meant being able to return to normal temperatures. It might be fun to explore Cornwall.

But the last night camping out in the desert turned out far better than imagined. The dry heat of the day faded away with the darkening skies. With the brilliant stars as a backdrop, Graham managed to photograph the impressive limestone formations called the Pinnacles. It would be perfect for his tales of wanderlust and sacred journeys.

It had helped him to clear his mind as well. Something about staring up at the vast dark sky filled with twinkling lights brought him peace. The weight of romantic mistakes from years ago seemed to sink into the sand under his feet and out of his soul.

Maybe I can forgive myself all the mistakes I've made. Maybe.

When Graham had been incredibly young and foolish, he had trodden all over the sensitive heart of a boyfriend, and it had changed him. He'd been altered by the knowledge that his callous actions had almost permanently harmed someone.

So many years had gone by. Maybe it was finally time to let it go. He could release himself from the guilt of it all.

"Excited to be heading home?" His guide broke through his thoughts.

Graham lifted his mug of tea that admittedly looked, smelled, and tasted more like Tooheys than tea to salute the man who had been with him for the past week. "I'd be more thrilled if you hadn't forced me to try Vegemite."

"Breakfast of champions."

"Vile. Disgusting. Useless." Graham hated Vegemite. He grimaced over the rim of his mug of beer. No, tea, definitely tea. He patted his chest to attempt to relieve yet another bout of indigestion. "Might need a top-up to wash the taste from my mouth."

CHAPTER TWO

Dark blue, almost black eyes stared into dark brown ones. Neither blinked. Neither budged an inch. Twenty minutes of staring and BC hadn't managed to get Zeus to budge.

Who names a bloody ankle-biter after a god?

Judas Priest.

Is this what I'm reduced to? Glaring at a five-pound Yorkie to get off my bed? If Uncle Davie hadn't died, I'd bring the bastard back to kick him in the arse for leaving me his mangy mutt. What the bloody hell do I do with this thing?

"Stop staring at me, you flea-infested mongrel." BC threw his arms up in the air in frustration when the dog simply curled up on his pillow and started snoring. "Defeated by a mutt no bigger than a potato. *Brilliant.*"

He collapsed back on the bed with a thump, smirking

when it jolted Zeus slightly. His amusement faded when he realised the mattress had to be a good six inches too short for his six-foot-seven frame.

Why me?

Then again, it's not the most awkward place I've slept, is it?

In his early years in the rugby world, BC could recall sleeping in awkward positions on trains, buses, and even in locker rooms. He'd slept underneath a bench once after a night out at the pub.

Good memories. Clinging to those kept him from growing too depressed by his situation. He shifted around on the lumpy mattress, attempting to find a comfortable position.

Shoving the overly flowery quilt to the side, BC dragged his tired body off the uncomfortable bed. He'd clearly grown too old to sleep any and everywhere. Thirty-four didn't seem ancient, though it certainly felt it at times.

For all his immense muscle and strength, he felt ancient and broken. Losing his spot on the national rugby union team's touring squad after a string of muscle strains that resulted in poor performances in key matches had cost him his confidence and eventually his career. Running away in disgrace had seemed the only recourse.

Uncle Davie's bed and breakfast on a cliff near Whitsand Bay had granted him a chance to retreat even further. Failure didn't come gracefully to the Brooks men. He hated it as his father had before him, loathed it more than spiders and flying combined, his two greatest fears.

Spiders. The eight-legged bastards.

The inn named the Fisherman's Refuge had scores of them high up in the corners waiting to drop on his head. He tried to remind himself they could be crushed by his thumb. It didn't help—at all.

Spiders. If all his troubles could be trampled like arachnids, BC thought life might take a turn for the better. A quick glance around the dark room reassured him none threatened him with immediate doom. Bloody things.

With a scratch to his side, BC stretched out his sore muscles. He ran his fingertips across the tribal rugby rose tattooed upon his chest. It had been inked years ago when so many promising things still seemed possible, before the sport he'd loved since childhood had broken his heart.

"Oh, for the love of God, stop moaning, you numpty." BC cursed his continued moping. "It's naffing done, isn't it? Can't change it now."

A yip from Zeus told him perhaps it might be time to cease talking to himself. He needed a distraction, a bigger one than the inn and the smirking Yorkie staring at him from the bed. Time to get on with his life, one without rugby, fame, and glory in it.

Using moonlight from the windows to navigate the narrow halls, BC made his way through the inn. It had been a boarding house in the seventeenth century belonging to one of his ancestors, which had been passed down from one generation of Brookses to the next. His grandmother had chosen to renovate it from its stark interior into a cosy seaside bed and breakfast in the forties.

When Uncle Davie inherited it in the seventies, he

had done yet another renovation and had modernised it one last time a few years ago in time for the London Olympics in the hopes of garnering a few guests. A local Cornwall designer, Francis, had managed the job, turning the place into a picturesque cottage-style inn with all updated modern comforts.

Good old Francis.

BC had met the younger man through an old rugby mate, Caddock. He had even attended their wedding last year, along with the rest of their former teammates. Seeing everyone had only served to increase his resentment at his circumstances.

Thinking about the wedding brought him back to that brief moment in the closet. *Ahh, Graham.* The man intrigued him, and his sudden disappearance to parts unknown had only increased his interest.

Who didn't love a good mystery? A mystery he wanted to thoroughly unravel. *Thoroughly fuck as well.* He'd always had a thing for gingers.

Their brief moment together had sparked something in him. He'd thought all the weight of disappointment had killed his joy, but that one brief fling in a church closet had breathed new life into him.

The second meeting, when BC had approached Rupert for help with the inn, had been highly entertaining. Graham had clearly expected to never see him again. He'd gotten a good laugh at the panic in the man's eyes.

He'd planned it out with Rupert over the phone. Graham had been tricked into spending time with his twin.

His eyes had gone wide when BC showed up.

Rupert had also been highly entertained by his normally smooth-talking brother stumbling over his words. The torture hadn't lasted long. Graham had made a quick escape out of his brother's office and likely out of the country, as well.

It wouldn't be easy to pin Graham down. He remembered a conversation with Rupert about his travelling twin brother who would disappear for weeks and months at a time. Maybe it was time to get over his fear of flying.

But first.

First, the inn had to get up and running, Zeus had to be handled, and his beard needed a trim. Scruffy didn't look good on him. He tended to look more thuggish than anything when he hadn't shaved, not something to entice a travelling writer.

Well? You want him. Get yourself up and go get him. Graham Hodson won't want a sobbing, whinging boy. You're older. Wiser. Time to show it.

CHAPTER THREE

GRAHAM

"You could've stayed with us, you great lummox." Rupert wandered around the small place his brother had leased from a family friend. "You could've asked me for help."

The flat had everything Graham would need, which honestly wasn't much. A bed, a space to write, a shower. What else did a single bloke who'd be out and about really want in a living space? *Nothing.*

Ignoring his twin, Graham grabbed the bags of clothing that had been stored at his parents' house while travelling. He had a brilliant flat in London, but he wouldn't be returning to it until the Cornwall series had been written, maybe not even then, as a trip to Palau beckoned after this. Jellyfish Lake would make for an interesting story—and a nerve-racking swim.

"Stop it." Rupert swatted him over the head with a folded T-shirt before dropping it into the wardrobe. "You can't swan off before you've seen everyone. Have you even visited the places you're supposed to be writing about? I heard Whitsand Bay Beach is on the top of your list. You might consider staying at the Fisherman's Refuge."

The Fisherman's Refuge?

Why does that name sound so familiar?

"You arse." Graham spun around to face his brother, shaking a pair of trousers that wasn't nearly as threatening or satisfying as he wanted it to be. "You talked to Becca."

Rebekah Jones, one of the senior editors at the magazine, was a close friend to his sister-in-law. He wouldn't put it past his arse of a brother to try to find a way to throw him together with Boyce Brooks, if only to humiliate him. They'd always enjoyed taking the mickey out of one another whenever possible.

Shit.

"Booked you a room for three nights. Enjoy." Rupert dodged the articles of clothing being flung at him. "Is this the thanks I get for trying to give you a welcome home present?"

"I'll give you a present—my boot up your arse." Graham hunted for something heavier and harder to launch at his twin, only to look up to see Rupert had already escaped. "Bastard."

Giving up on the concept of unpacking now that it would all be going back in his bag, Graham prepared himself mentally for days spent in close proximity to temptation. One he had hoped to resist if at all possible. Romantic complications were definitely not a welcome intrusion in his life.

Two options stood before him: pretend to be oblivious to the situation, or face things head-on like an adult. He usually preferred to avoid grown-up responsibilities. Rupert could handle that as the older twin.

Oblivious it is.

Three days wouldn't be hard. Right? The Fisherman's Refuge had enough rooms for there to be at least one or two other guests. He could use them as a barrier.

His travel bag sat on the edge of his rented bed, mocking him. It still needed a clear-out after his last trip. He'd left it rather full of TimTam wrappers and bottle caps from the numerous brands of beer he'd tried in Australia—for research purposes, of course.

Oh, the sacrifices I make for my articles.

With rainy and brisk weather on the horizon, he knew warm-weather attire would be out. Of the twins, Rupert had always been the one who cared more about his appearance than the simple function of his clothes. Graham wasn't trying to impress anyone in any case.

Grabbing his bag, he tilted it up and began shaking it over the rubbish bin to rid it of the refuse left over from his travels. The old leather travel pack had served him well. He plonked it on the bed with a sigh and started to reach for clothes to toss inside.

His mobile gave a merry jingle, and he scrambled through the mass of items on the bed to find it. He answered without bothering to glance at the number. "Hodson."

A familiar female voice with the slightest hint of a

French accent came through. "Has he told you?"

"Et tu, Brute?" Graham glared even though Becca wouldn't see it to appreciate the depth of his annoyance. Her accent came from her time spent with her French mother. Her looks, however, had been inherited from her father's family, who had come from one of the many Caribbean island nations. "Of course he told me. Would my bastard twin wait to needle me with information guaranteed to torture me?"

"You'll thank me later."

"Goodbye, Becca."

"Wear your green shirt, the long-sleeved one Mama sent you from her last trip to Paris. It brings out your eyes," she offered helpfully, her amusement clear in her melodic voice, also inherited from her mother. "We can chat about your upcoming article later."

She meant gossip about BC. He knew it. She wouldn't be able to resist wanting to know every detail.

"*Bye.*" Graham tossed the phone to the side.

She'd been trying to fix him up for ages. Everyone always attempted to pair him off with someone. He could only hope they gave up eventually.

Another reason to constantly flee to the far corners of the earth. He hadn't expected all those in his life to suddenly become co-conspirators on the issue. Didn't they all have lives of their own to lead? Well, if he did decide to wear a certain shirt in a certain colour, Becca's nosy nonsense would have nothing to do with it.

Nothing.

I could wear the green shirt. I could. It wouldn't hurt,

would it?

What soppy shit is this?

He didn't want or need a man in his life. He didn't. Sex wouldn't be bad, though. It had been a few months, and his hand might develop calluses soon if he didn't branch out.

Fine. The green shirt it is. Becca doesn't need to know.

Did things like the shade of his shirt actually matter? Francis thought it did, but he was dandier than Beau Brummel and Lord Byron combined. His childhood friend could pull off bow ties and suspenders while Graham could barely tie his own boots.

His old things had served him well. They had scrapes, scuffs, and dirt from all over the planet. He treasured them almost as much as he did the stamps in his passport.

The passport stamps he loved so much had been tattooed across his back in the shape of a jumbo jet. His mum had been horrified when she'd seen the multicoloured artwork. *Job well done.* She generally found everything about his life choices shocking.

"Why don't you settle down like your brother?"

He'd get right on it. Why would he want to be a boring ginger working in an office when he could be the adventurous twin? He loved his life; maybe it tended to be lonely at times, but he'd chosen to make those sacrifices.

So, shirt, bag, boots. Time to go. And trousers, people tended to not approve of wandering around in undies, socks, and a shirt. It might distract everyone from his love life, though.

Nah. Not worth the shit it would cause. Trousers it is. Maybe a haircut first. I wonder if Jack's busy.

CHAPTER FOUR

BC

Judas Priest.

If there had been hair to yank on his head, BC would've made himself bald already. Zeus had taken a piss on yet another pair of shoes. The Yorkie got a walk four times a day, yet it didn't seem to matter. The blasted dog hadn't taken well to his new owner and showed his displeasure in the smelliest of ways.

Mrs Beatrice Morgan, the woman who had run the inn for his uncle and now ran it for him, assured him that Zeus would settle into a new routine eventually. It took a Herculean effort not to comment on the ease of the statement when it wasn't her shoes playing loo to the Yorkie. He'd soon run out of trainers at this rate.

Was there such a thing as doggie therapy?

The old inn had a week break coming up with only one guest, so he'd told Mrs Morgan to take a few days to visit with her grandkids. Better to have the entire place to himself when Graham arrived. The only potential issue left to deal with was the fur-covered one.

After making sure the room next to his was set up for his guest, BC hopped into the shower to get a quick wash-up. He made sure to touch up the close shave of his beard. His hair tended to grow far too quickly for his liking.

His fingers fumbled with the laces of his trainers while the bell downstairs rang repeatedly. Boyce had planned for a strong first impression—well, not first, but a strong one all the same. He didn't, however, foresee slipping on dog mess on the staircase and thudding his way down the last six steps.

"You *bastard* of a mongrel. I'll skin you. Turn you into mincemeat." BC caught his breath, lying flat on his back. He gritted his teeth when the bell rang again. "Keep your knickers on, I'm getting there."

"You sure about that?" Graham sounded highly amused.

"Have you seen a four-legged monster?" BC lifted his head from where it had gotten wedged against the last stair and the wall. "Dog left a gift for me on the stairs."

"Puts a new turn on being shit-faced."

Well. Shit. It happens, right? Get off the floor, you numpty.

"Less fun." BC pushed himself to his feet. He grimaced at the mess on his jeans and the stairs. "Kitchen's down to the right. Grab tea while I clean this all up."

Another shower. A better shirt. One quick swig of the

scotch his uncle had kept hidden in a secret compartment on his bed frame for courage. Time to get it right, without dog shit and the fall down the stairs.

The object of his affection and the focus of his aggravation had joined one another in the kitchen. Zeus sat on a stool while Graham fed him part of a biscuit. *Judas Priest.* Did the furry little bastard have to charm the man so quickly?

BC glared at the Yorkie, who didn't even blink at him. "We're going to have words later."

Graham snorted into his tea in obvious amusement. "Do you often lecture dogs smaller than the rugby ball you used to throw around?"

"Only recently." BC decided the best course of action would be to ignore both man and beast for the moment. He moved towards the kettle, returning it to the range to make his own cup. "You won't find it as funny when the little twit is taking a piss on your things in the middle of the night."

"I've had worse." Graham shrugged.

BC couldn't help but blink in surprise. "Really?"

"Tell you about it over a pint." He closed his eyes for a moment as if berating himself for something. "If you like."

"Room first?"

For men who had canoodled in a closet at a wedding, BC thought they couldn't be more awkward if they tried. At this rate, he should've let Mrs Morgan stay. She couldn't have cock-blocked him any more effectively than he was doing himself.

Get. On. With. It. You. Numpty.

"Take your bag for you?" BC had to suddenly resist the

urge to bash his skull into the nearby antique china cabinet. Graham smirked at him, and he couldn't help returning the grin. "Since we all but buggered each other at Caddock's nuptials, how about we skip the awkward 'pretending it's the first time we've met' shit?"

"Agreed." Graham's smile broadened, making him far more roguish than should've been possible. "Do you always drag charming men into dark corners at weddings?"

"Only the gingers."

"Bastard."

"My parents might not have been overly happy together, but they were definitely married when I popped out." BC chugged down the last bit of his tea and set the mug in the sink for later. He spared one last glare at the furry creature happily accepting love from the slightly smaller and slightly younger man. "I hope he takes a wee on your head in the middle of the night."

"Do I have to pay extra for it?"

"Cheeky bastard." BC waved him out of the kitchen to show him to his room.

Leaving the wandering journalist to get settled in comfortably, BC took Zeus for a fourth walk—just in case. His mission to confidently seduce the man had gone to pot, but hopefully it wouldn't be a total wash. He needed a better plan.

Time to regroup.

Zeus scampered along the path that led down from the inn to the beach. He'd never been one for pets. His uncle had written him a letter in the will, asking him to care for his beloved canine as his own.

Weren't dogs supposed to help with romance? Zeus had been nothing but a complete nightmare thus far. He'd think it couldn't get worse, but that would be begging for trouble.

He tripped over the leash and almost went headlong down the path to his death.

Bloody dog in his bloody sweater, so he doesn't freeze. Why me?

CHAPTER FIVE

GRAHAM

The Fisherman's Refuge had turned out to have all the charm one would expect from a Cornwall bed and breakfast. Francis had done a brilliant job in designing it to evoke all the long-forgotten nostalgia of holidays by the sea. It made him want to lose his lunch all over the antique rose quilt on the bed.

Flowers. Antique white. Old wood and copper.

Old things that smelled old. He'd never understand why Francis enjoyed antique hunting. Dusty and mouldy. His friend could have the lot. He'd rather sleep under the stars than with creepy dolls and doilies.

Old. Old. Old.

Tossing his bag on the high-backed chair in the corner, Graham moved over to the large windows. On the beach below, he could barely make out the lumbering form of BC with the tiny speck of Zeus beside him. He couldn't help but sink down on the edge of the mattress, laughing at the absurdity of it.

He fumbled for his mobile and then darted back to the window to get a quick video, which he immediately sent out to Jack, Francis, and Rupert. They always shared moments of absurdity for a good laugh. If nothing else, the weekend would provide plenty of them. A bloke could earn free pints of beer with a good story or three—names changed to protect the guilty, of course.

His text from Jack thanked him for "cheering me up after another dreadful date." Graham had no idea why the man even bothered to try anymore. He had to have the worst luck when it came to dating of anyone in the world. It was always one bad experience after another.

Why did anyone even bother with anything but fleeting romances nowadays? Love seemed such a bother, not worth the trouble or the drama. He'd seen enough of it with his brother's wooing of his first fiancée, which ended in broken hearts for both of them.

He knew why. Hope. It always came down to starry-eyed dreams of blissful companionship into old age. The lying tits merely ignored the statistics on all the failed attempts to get to that magical state. He'd yet to meet someone who made the pain of having love-tinged shards of glass shoved through the heart worth it.

It wasn't.

Sod any twit who disagrees.

The annoying voice in his head, which sounded

remarkably like his twin, told him perhaps the vehemence of his argument betrayed a bit of defensiveness. It—and his brother—could take a long swim in the sea on a very cold day. Despite the turmoil, his eyes strayed down to the figures on the path below.

Don't even think about it.

Sex.

It would only be sex. Nothing wrong with that, after all. Good sex and lots of it, before he swanned off to his next adventure. He could never visit Cornwall for long without wanderlust setting in, and his need to travel overcame everything else.

I wonder how many surfaces in the inn we can christen before I leave.

Not the bedrooms; the duvet alone would give him nightmares for weeks. It certainly wouldn't get him in an amorous mood. All the fabric did was remind him of his nan; Graham shuddered, the mere thought banishing even the hint of romance.

A jaunty beep from his mobile drew his attention to happier things. It seemed Rupert had forwarded the video to *all* of his old rugby buddies. BC would be fit to be tied when they all reached out to him to take the mickey, and they definitely would.

A second message followed his twin's first.

Rupert: Don't be afraid to try—you broke one heart, not enough of a reason to seal your own off for the rest of your life.

Only Rupert. Ever the optimist and ever a pain in the

arse, he always worked to try to help everyone find happiness, or at least ensure a good laugh was had by all. His brother probably hoped a connection with BC would keep Graham closer to home.

He didn't *want* to make a life in Cornwall. Staying in one place for more than a month usually had him itching to take a trip anywhere that required getting on a plane. He was happiest living out of his kit bag, wandering from one adventure to another.

Joanne had once told him to find someone who loved to travel. No one in his family seemed to understand that it never bothered him to travel alone. Happiness to him came in a new stamp in his passport and finding new places to explore.

The idea that his family thought he required a partner to be satisfied was rather insulting. He didn't. It might be nice, but the world wouldn't fall to pieces if nothing other than casual interludes came his way.

And neither will I.

"Settled in then?"

Graham couldn't quite stop the slight jolt of surprise. "Not much to settle. I've never been one to pack or unpack. It all stays in the bag."

"Wrinkly, but convenient." BC picked up the camera that Graham had taken the time to unpack. "Do you enjoy the travel, the photography, or the food the most?"

"All of the above?" Graham reached into his bag to retrieve the large journal that he used as a travel diary. It contained sketches, notes, and photos. He tossed it over to BC and sat cross-legged on the bed. "I have one for each year since I started."

He flipped through the pages slowly. "I'm terrified of flying."

Graham blinked once… twice before shaking his head with a wry smile. "Really? Why?"

"No idea. It doesn't seem safe, floating around like a tin of sardines." He continued perusing the journal with what at least appeared to be an interested gleam in his eyes. "Cornwall must pale in comparison to some of these places."

"It's home."

"And home looks best from a distance?"

Graham couldn't help but laugh at the painful truth of the simple statement. "It does. It makes attempting to write about it difficult."

"Cornwall must seem exotic to visitors, though. Why don't you attempt to see the sights and taste the food through a stranger's eyes?" BC gently closed the book in his hands and set it to the side. "How about we start with Mrs Morgan's saffron buns? She left a batch of them."

"Saffron buns?" He couldn't keep the incredulity out of his voice. "I haven't had one of those since my nan used to make them for afternoon tea. My parents fobbed us off on her on weekends when they'd grown tired of corralling their troublesome twins."

"I can always eat them all myself." BC shrugged.

"You sure?" Graham found himself torn between laughter and intrigue. "Saffron buns it is."

"Why don't we play tourists during your stay?" BC commented randomly.

His first instinct was to say no and explain how much he preferred to explore alone. The words never left his mouth. Graham heard himself saying, "Yes, why not?" It was the closest to an out-of-body experience he'd ever had.

"Where should we start?" Graham shook his head to gather his scattered thoughts together.

"Saffron buns." BC appeared the picture of innocence.

"After the buns?" He couldn't help the twitch of his lips at the last word. "Buns."

BC's shoulders shook with laughter. "*Buns.*"

CHAPTER SIX

BC

Cooking supper had been a terrible idea. Graham had hopped up casually on a barstool he'd dragged into the kitchen to watch the unfolding chaos. He now sat, hunched over in laughter, not even attempting to hide his amusement as tears streamed from his eyes.

"It's not *that* funny." BC took the ruined pans from the range and threw them into the sink with a disgusted grimace. "Will you stop laughing?"

"It really, truly is *that* funny." Graham wiped his eyes with his sleeve, still chuckling. "How do you muck up beans on toast? It's heating up the beans and dropping bread in the toaster. You are shit in the kitchen."

BC wanted to argue, but couldn't help his own bark of laughter. "I swear I know how to cook."

Graham straightened himself up and grabbed his mobile. He had a whispered conversation with someone before turning to BC with a smile. "An old school mate runs the Canteen at Maker Heights. It's closed in the evenings, but he'll brave the icy weather to bring us some of their leftovers."

The leftovers turned out to be roast pork sarnies, pickled pear salad, and a lightly curried parsnip soup. The chef had been kind enough to add a small container of chocolate-covered hokey pokey, which Graham snatched up. He'd crunched his way through half of the honeycomb treats before BC could get even one of them.

"Do you always eat dessert first?"

"Always."

BC swatted his hands away from the container to grab himself a few more of the roughly square-shaped treats after setting out the rest of the food on the table. "So where should we start our grand adventure tomorrow?"

"Pasties."

"Pardon?"

"Not the nipple covers, mind you, the pastries. We should discover where to find the best pasties in Cornwall." Graham grinned cheekily at him with honeycomb crumbs on his bottom lip. "My editor sent a list of all the bakeries within easy driving distance. Up for a challenge?"

The flecks of golden honeycomb taunted BC. He wanted a taste of both the treat and Graham. He'd never been one to deny himself anything.

BC reached a long, muscled arm across the table to grab a surprised Graham by the neck. He tugged him up across the table and took his time licking the sweet crumbs from his lips. "I'm always up for a challenge."

"Good. Your shirt's seasoning the soup."

Judas Priest.

"Easily fixed." BC grabbed his shirt and yanked it over his head, tossing it to the side with a careless grace. He hid his smile when Graham's gaze drifted down his chest. "Like the view?"

Graham gestured to the tattoo on his side. "I'd forgotten we have the same ink."

Those green eyes *hadn't* been focused on his side for long. He'd bet all the money the inn earned in the next year that the tattoos had been the last thing on Graham's mind. It took an immense amount of self-control to avoid flexing his muscles and showing off a bit.

Why bother? My body speaks for itself, doesn't it?

"So pasties?" BC sat down, reaching for a plate to fill up, nonchalant as if he weren't bare chested. "Why don't we organise the list based on distance? We can visit them in order. How many of them are there?"

"Thirty?"

"Maybe not all in one day." He had a sudden vision of them swimming in meat pasties. "I have a distinct feeling we'll be well shot of them by the time we get to the last one on the list."

"Might be well shot of each other." Graham dipped his spoon into the soup for a taste. "You sure you want to join me?"

"Wouldn't miss it." BC nodded.

He meant it as well. The short time spent with Graham so far had been great fun; it would be a shame to give it up so soon. Why stop a good thing?

With Graham's bright green eyes occasionally straying towards his upper body, BC stayed shirtless. It obviously wouldn't hurt his attempts at seduction. Any advantage at this point was a good thing.

A yip from under the table pulled his attention to the major hindrance to his relaxing. The blasted dog was grabbing his trousers between his teeth and tugging on them. He'd fed the animal already, and walked the damn thing. What else could it possibly want now?

If his Uncle Davie ever returned as a ghostly spectre, BC would be sure to ask the man what he had done to deserve punishment in the form of a deranged Yorkie. Before he could do anything, Graham had reached down and lifted the mutt up to set him on a chair. The cheeky bugger of a dog immediately curled up and started to snore.

They finished dinner in a companionable silence broken only by the snuffling of Zeus. Graham smirked at him whenever BC glared at the dog. He appeared to find his irritation entertaining.

His struggles with the mini-mutt was, if nothing else, completely absurd, and BC could appreciate a love of silliness. He had an obsessive love for Monty Python, after all.

Noshing on some of the morsels of sugary shards remaining, he prompted his dinner companion to share more of his stories of his travels. As someone who had never travelled much beyond rugby matches, he found it all fascinating. It made him want to brave his phobia of flight to experience more of the world—almost.

BC could easily imagine why he had taken to travel writer so brilliantly. Graham definitely came alive in his role of storyteller. The redhead had a gift for weaving tales, and he could honestly have listened to him for hours on end without complaint.

Being so handsome didn't hurt matters either. The younger man had such piercing green eyes that BC found himself constantly drawn into them. He wanted more than his earlier stolen kiss, a lot more.

"Where do you want to travel next?" BC asked after a prolonged silence where the quiet had settled around them as a comforting warmth.

"Finland."

"Why?"

"I'm hoping to wrap up my Cornwall story by the middle of March. If I manage it, I can make it out to Kakslauttanen. I could see the Northern Lights, stay in a glass igloo, and freeze my arse off in the Arctic Circle." Graham grabbed the travel journal he'd brought out to show photos earlier. He flipped towards the empty pages at the back and twisted it around to show a page with the beginnings of an entry. "I've kept a spot for it in every diary I've kept since I began writing. I always seem to miss out on the season, since it runs from August to April. Either the season ends early, or I have other places to visit. This is the year, though, I've promised myself."

"Have you?" BC stretched a hand out to run a finger along the mostly empty page. "Are you sure you'll be up for all the ice and snow?"

"I'm sure you'll find I'm up for many things." Graham grinned at him before closing his journal. "Let's watch a movie."

CHAPTER SEVEN

GRAHAM

Aside from his twin brother, Graham had never laughed as much with another person as he'd done with BC. They'd spent the remainder of the night munching on honeycomb and watching Monty Python—both *The Meaning of Life* and *The Holy Grail*. Kisses had been traded, stolen really, between bites of the sweet shards.

Only kisses.

Pity.

It seemed silly, given their sojourn in the closet at the wedding, not to simply indulge themselves sexually. BC had been surprisingly reticent. Graham couldn't figure out why, though the mischievous twinkle in the man's eyes made him wonder what he had planned.

Graham's only consolation was they'd both gone to bed

hard and unsatisfied. BC hadn't stayed that way if the sounds coming from his room were anything to go by. He appeared to take great joy in pleasuring himself as loudly as possible.

The bastard.

Any other time, he would've found it equal parts hilarious and annoying to listen in on someone else and their solitary sexual release. The inn's thin walls allowed him to hear every nuance of BC's breathing. His own shaft hardened further with each passing moment and moan.

His self-control didn't stretch to not joining in himself, however. Graham collapsed back on the chair in his room, naked in the moonlight shining through the window. His fingers glided easily over the already sensitive head of his cock.

Over the course of his sexual adventures, Graham had enjoyed mutual satisfaction with others, but it had never happened quite like this—or felt so incredibly sensually enticing. He could almost imagine the fingers on him weren't his own.

Eyes closed. Fingers loosely stroked up and down. His breath caught in his throat while his body tightened with need, so much of it.

A wall might separate the two of them, but it felt as if they were sitting across from each other. Graham's fingers travelled a familiar path, touching the most sensitive areas with practised skill. He could easily visualise BC mimicking his actions nearby.

Up. Down. Up down.

Slickness eased the glide of his hand. With a muted cry,

Graham spurted onto his stomach and fingers. He heard BC find his release not long after.

He chose to ignore the tinny howl from Zeus. BC's call of "sleep well, Ginger Spice" was infinitely more difficult to brush off. Pretending not to hear seemed the best of his choices.

Ginger Spice?

I'll show the arse some spice in the morning.

Two can play the teasing game.

Despite the snarky predictions of the previous day, Zeus didn't pop into his room during the night to leave smelly gifts. Graham woke up surprisingly well-rested and excited to take on the day. A tray with coffee and something vaguely resembling a scone had been left outside his door.

The scone had been voraciously attacked by something—likely a fur-covered menace. Zeus appeared to have eaten the cream but left the jam and raisins from the scone. The coffee seemed unscathed, or at least free of hair.

Gulping down the tepid liquid, Graham plotted out his plans for the morning. A shower, breakfast—preferably one not chewed by others—and most importantly, an opportunity to repay the teasing from the previous night. He didn't think it would be too difficult to manage.

A burp caught him by surprise. Graham rubbed absently at his chest. His indigestion had gotten worse lately. No matter what he ate, it seemed to give him problems.

He'd eaten his way through what felt like a ton of Tums. Becca had imported them for him. They helped, a little.

Less and less, actually.

Bloody inconvenient.

He glanced out the window after a quick shower and discovered a jacket would be required. Cornish Februarys could be bitingly cold and brisk. He suddenly regretted borrowing Joanne's Porsche, not a vehicle suited for snowy days and icy roads.

"You alive in there?" BC called from outside the door. "Was the coffee warm enough?"

"Define warm." Graham yanked on his trousers and shoved his socked feet into his boots. He tied the laces up quickly and grabbed his backpack, which held both his camera and journal for notes. He yanked the door open to find a grinning BC waiting. "Zeus enjoyed the scone."

"*Shit.*"

"No, none of that despite your threats." He followed the larger man through the narrow hall and down towards the kitchen. "Ready to brave the cold in the name of pasties?"

BC lifted his mug in salute. "Over the top with us."

"Twit."

A quick nosh on the rest of the scones that Mrs Morgan had brought over, and the two men hopped in BC's Mercedes SLS Roadster, a vehicle only slightly worse than a Porsche for winter travel. They'd plotted out a path from Torpoint along the A30 through Bodmin, Truro, and several other villages before stopping in Kynance Cove Beach, one of the places on Rebekah's list for him to visit.

Though the drive to Kynance should've taken less than an hour, they managed to make it to the cove in five hours with all the stopping. Six bakers, twelve pasties, six scones, four Bakewell tarts, and umpteen other pastries later, Graham felt a bit food-logged and decidedly sleepy by the time the rocky cliffs came into view. He didn't think his drowsy mind could do the place justice.

The rare falling snow made it even more picturesque with the rough wind and water-hewn rocky outcroppings that made up the small inlet. The snow wasn't enough to even linger, melting before it hit the ground, but Graham still grabbed his camera to take a few photos. Between the pasties and Kynance, he had enough to write at least three articles.

"Oi, Ginger Spice, you up for skinny-dipping?"

Graham stared at BC for a few seconds, wondering if he'd lost his mind. They'd made a quick visit to an antique bookstore while taking a break from the pasties; he'd spotted the former rugby player with his nose in a first edition Jerome K. Jerome, actually smelling the pages. "Sure, book sniffer. It's only snowing and a few degrees off my bollocks freezing, perfect weather for diving in the sea."

"I was not sniffing books, you numpty," he protested far too vehemently. "Stop grinning at me."

"The first step to recovery is admitting you have a problem." Graham smiled even wider. "No judgement, I promise."

"*Bastard.*" BC kicked sand up at him. "So? You up for it?"

Skinny-dipping in the middle of the afternoon in February where anyone and their gran might see?

Not the stupidest shit I've ever done.

"We get arrested, I'm claiming you threatened to pound

me into the sand." Graham narrowed his eyes when the man grinned. "Not like that, you plonker."

"Whatever you say, Ginger Spice."

"Book sniffer." Graham toed off his boots, not bothering to untie his laces. "Better make it quick, someone might notice two pale arses running around Kynance Cove."

"You think?"

"Pants?"

The briefs thrown into his face answered his question. He wondered absently if Rebekah would want him to include this little adventure in his articles—with or without photographic evidence. A side glance at BC told him perhaps it might be more pornographic than anything else.

Why are we doing this? This is stupid. Oh, he's naked. Never mind, it's brilliant.

Bloody hell, it's bigger than I remember, even in the Arctic. Not feeling inadequate—not feeling inadequate.

With a wink, BC practically tackled him into the icy water. The sudden rush of brisk air paled in comparison to the biting cold of the sea. *Shit.* Graham could feel his important bits shrivelling up and dying in protest.

Starting to make a move to get out of the sea, Graham found himself caught by a strong arm around his waist. He was pulled over until his body lined up with BC's. His six-two stature didn't match the impressive six foot seven inches of the larger man.

Fingers gripped a clump of his formerly gelled hair, tilting his head back for a kiss. They inhaled almost in unison when a wave sent chilly water up higher. Another kiss, another flash of heat, then whistling from up on the cliff told them the time had come to get back in their clothes.

Silence reigned inside the Mercedes while they made a quick getaway. The chuckles from the older couple who had been walking their wolfhound hadn't dampened their spirits at all. The wife, who had been in her seventies at least, gave them two thumbs up that had BC struggling to keep his laughter in check until they'd gotten safely to the car.

"Was that a life goal or something?" Graham rubbed his hands up and down his arms.

"Of course, being old and still able to have a laugh. Top of my list." BC reached over to flip up the heater to full whack. "How're your bollocks?"

"Frozen."

Grabbing his journal, Graham jotted down snippets of what would become a full journal. He sketched out an outline for the other one, and pasties, *shit*, if he had to eat one more damn meat pie today. Tomorrow would be more of the same; the things he suffered for his work.

He couldn't help but shiver despite the rapidly warming vehicle. The icy ocean had chilled him down to the bone. He hoped this adventure hadn't put him at risk for a silly cold, or worse, hypothermia. Rebekah would never let him hear the end of it if she found out.

"How about we stop at a pub for dinner?" Graham didn't want to risk more pastry, not today. "I could use a beer, or three."

BC chuckled a little too knowingly before responding. "No more pasties? I've got a better idea."

"Not sure I could handle your attempt to cook again." Graham was certain he could still smell burnt food. "Are you *trying* to kill your guest with food poisoning?"

"Don't be difficult, Ginger Spice." He smacked him on the arm and then turned his attention to getting the vehicle going. "You'll see."

CHAPTER EIGHT

BC

BC watched Graham continue to shiver out of the corner of his eyes despite the heat pouring out of the vent, and knocked the temperature up a few degrees to help warm him up. "Going to include skinny-dipping in your writing?"

"No." Graham spoke through his chattering teeth. "Maybe. Might recommend avoiding it in the middle of sodding winter."

When BC had mentioned wanting to wine and dine someone, Caddock had offered a few helpful suggestions for restaurants—after discussing it with his husband. One of the suggestions had been for a little place called Ben's Cornish Kitchen. It sounded a bit posh, but why not? He drove north, hopefully in time for the table that Francis had booked for them.

Over the starter of smoked duck breast with some sort of wine that seemed far too expensive to his mind, BC discovered Graham had visited every continent on the planet. He also appeared to have no favourite places. *Surprising.* It was the actual exploring the man enjoyed the most, discovering different foods, people, and cultures.

They moved on to pan fried hake, greens, and gnocchi. Boyce had never enjoyed a meal or a companion more. Even if Graham did periodically toss chunks of food at him, and he did return the favour a few times, much to the annoyance of the staff.

Must remember to add a fair chunk to the bill by way of apology.

The two men snickered their way through a trifle and a sweet port. Cream ended up on Graham's nose and BC's ear. They found it convenient to lick it off, leaving them more than ready for the drive back to the inn when the manager kicked them out for being indecent.

Ready might've actually been a strong word. BC hadn't expected the man sitting to his left to suddenly develop a case of wandering fingers. He'd been focusing on getting safely back on the A30 when a hand dropped perilously close to the centre of his lap.

Cheeky bugger.

Avoiding taking them off the road into a hedge, or worse, off a cliff, had proven far more difficult than anticipated. He kept one hand on the steering wheel and let his other return the teasing favour. His roadster strayed across lanes several times, but thankfully not long enough to drive headlong into oncoming traffic.

"You're explaining this to the coppers if we get pulled over." BC impressed himself with the steadiness of his voice when those skilled fingers easily lowered his zipper and slipped inside his trousers. "I'll be the one claiming a sudden inability to think clearly, caused by too many strikes to the head during my career."

"Arse." Graham gave him a few tight squeezes before starting to stroke him again. "And how will you explain your fingers in *my* pants?"

"Amnesia."

"Don't think that word means what you think it does."

He could hear the laughter in Graham's voice without having to see his smirking face. "Doesn't matter if they believe me, does it?"

The teasing tugs between them continued for much of the drive. It made the hour fly by. He swerved into a somewhat decent parked position.

"In a hurry?" Graham asked amusedly, watching BC fumble for a second with the seat belt. "This is far too entertaining to accurately put into words—and I make a living using as many words as I can."

BC twisted in his seat and caught the redhead by the neck, hand firmly gripping him and dragging him into a kiss. His patience had come to an end; their lips crushed together, noses pressed against cheeks. He only pulled back when oxygen became a necessity. "Inside."

"Inside?"

"In-fucking-side." BC reached across to open

Graham's door. "I've had enough teasing for now."

The two men had the torturous wait of ensuring Zeus had been walked, again, and fed, before they settled the dog in his own room, for his sake and theirs. BC caught Graham by the back of his shirt to guide him down the hall into one of the larger rooms in the inn.

They stripped down to nothing in record time, sending sand leftover from their skinny-dip flying across the floor. BC had a brief, amusing image of explaining to Mrs Morgan how exactly it had gotten there. Graham moved forward, catching his attention immediately when he dragged their shafts against each other. BC twisted his hips from side to side; he couldn't help feel it was a bit like playing an amusing and erotic game of sword fighting—with very fleshy weapons.

"Always wanted to be a Jedi. Thought my lightsabre would be a tad longer." BC slid his fingers along the contours of the redhead's muscled abdomen. "Are you the chosen one?"

"You did *not* just—" Graham choked on his own saliva when laughter came bubbling up out of him. His breath still hitched when BC hit a sensitive spot. "*Shit.* The chosen one? Cheesiest. Line. Ever."

"Ever?" BC shook his head with a broad smile. "I'm confident I can do worse."

The laughter slowed down eventually, leaving the two men breathing heavily with their bodies barely an inch apart. One sway forward brushed him against the slightly smaller man. It did nothing to help regain any sense of control.

Done waiting. Done teasing. Done pretending I don't want to bugger him silly.

"Condoms?" Graham stopped him when he lifted his hands up to rest on his shoulders. "BC? Safe sex, or no fucking sex."

"Isn't fucking sex redundant?" He winced when Graham tweaked his nipple hard. "*Oi.* Keep your knickers on. Oh wait, you're not wearing any. I've got condoms somewhere."

"On your willy would be the preferred location." Graham smirked wickedly.

Can't disagree with that, can I?

Shaking his head and leaving Graham to laugh, BC made his way back to the room where Zeus had been *secured* to keep him out of trouble. He rifled through his bags until the stash of condoms and lube finally appeared. His relief at finding them was tangible, since it would've put a disappointing halt to their evening to have come up empty-handed.

He returned to find the naked journalist stretched out across the bed lazily stroking himself. "Success."

Graham gestured with his hand until the lube was tossed to him. "Watch."

The teasing had apparently *not* come to an end. BC's knees went weak while watching Graham prepare himself, and he sat on the edge of the bed to avoid hitting the floor. He'd brought his legs up, spreading them wide, and used lube-slicked fingers to stretch for his audience of one.

"Oh, yes." BC's eyes stayed glued to the three fingers drifting in and out, twisting around easily. "Just like that— ready for me, Ginger Spice?"

Catching the thrusting hand by the wrist, BC controlled the motion for several seconds before easing the fingers out. He kneeled on the mattress, looming over Graham and grabbing his legs to shift them up slightly for a better angle to torture them both as he sank into the sensual warmth with agonising slowness. Their noses brushed against each other's while they adjusted.

"Fucking. Brilliant," Graham muttered hoarsely before looping an arm around BC's neck, using it for leverage to work himself up and down. "So damn good."

The nipple inches from his mouth proved too tantalising to resist. BC captured it between his teeth, flicking his tongue across it repeatedly and enjoying the way that tight heat clenched around him as a result. Graham arched into his touch.

He brought his free hand up to slip a finger into the smaller man's mouth. He let Graham suck on it, laving it with his tongue repeatedly. "Not touching you—want you to come from me in you."

The fingers kept whatever narky response Graham had in check. BC used it to his advantage, pounding him into the mattress. He could feel the familiar tightening that signalled the cresting of their sought-after prize.

A sudden hard drive forward with a twist of a nipple brought Graham along for the ride. BC bucked wildly and then collapsed over on his side to avoid crushing the gasping journalist. They lay side by side, covered in sweat and grinning.

"The force is strong with you."

BC stripped off the used rubber and tossed it in the direction of the rubbish bin in the corner of the room. "Shut it, Ginger Spice."

CHAPTER NINE

GRAHAM

Smug was the one word to accurately describe the mood of the man lounging beside Graham in bed. BC hadn't moved post coitus, aside from grabbing a wet flannel to clean up any unpleasant leftover stickiness from their bodies. The only indication of his state of awareness came from his periodic satisfied sighs.

Smug arse.

"If you sigh one more bloody time." Graham grabbed the pillow from under his head and bludgeoned his bed partner with it when he gave an even longer exhalation.

"Judas Priest." BC rubbed his nose while glaring petulantly at Graham. "*Bastard.*"

A guttural shriek sent Graham flying off the bed a second later. BC stood hunched over on top of the corner bookshelf, all hulking two-hundred-sixty pounds of him, causing it to creak dangerously underneath him. The man shakily pointed towards the far corner of the ceiling where a spindly daddy-long-legs could be seen dangling.

"You have to be shitting me." Graham couldn't help the burble of mocking laughter that escaped him while he continued to watch the frantically gesturing former rugby player. "Are you actually telling me you're afraid of spiders?"

"Kill. It."

"All right, all right, keep your non-existent pants on." Graham had to strain to reach it, but at last managed to squash the tiny insect with a rolled newspaper. He briefly considered waving it at BC but tossed it in the rubbish bin instead—no point in being cruel. "So, eight-legged insects?"

"Should burn in hell."

"Right. The logical choice." Graham swallowed a snicker.

"Plotting evil bastards." BC continued to scowl in the direction of the now deceased creature.

"The spider?"

"Yes, you numpty, the evil insects might be tiny, but they plot our demise." BC finally unfolded himself from his improbable hiding spot on the bookshelf, thankfully before the wood snapped beneath him. "They are."

"*Right.*"

"So... tea?" BC cleared his throat and attempted to appear calm. "Scones? Maybe with clotted cream?"

Graham couldn't manage to hide his instinctual shudder. He didn't even like to hear the words clotted cream. They took him back to afternoons with his nan, who never checked the expiration dates on the stuff. "Tea is fine, no cream."

"No delicious Cornwall delicacy for your scone?"

"Would you like me to find a tarantula to drop on your head?" Graham decided to nip the teasing in the bud. "Maybe one prone to biting?"

"At least it would just be a flesh wound."

He gave a wry grin at the quote. "Up for another movie?"

It wouldn't be a date, Graham reasoned, only food, a movie, and maybe naughty things on the sofa. Not anything that would be construed as the start of a relationship. With only two days left before both the Fisherman's Refuge and BC would be left behind, he didn't see any harm in indulging.

They noshed on a cobbled-together snack of leftovers, with not a drop of freakishly thick cream in sight. Late night blended into early morning while they ate, told jokes, and laughed until they were delirious at the antics of the Monty Python crew. They fell asleep on the couch together after snogging themselves into an exhausted state, with Zeus stretched out between them.

Gentle licks to his hand woke him up. Graham had a brief moment of enjoying being brought to consciousness in such a pleasant manner until he realised the tongue belonged to the dog—not the owner of said creature. He found BC sacked out next to him and decided to forestall any issues by taking Zeus for his apparently much-needed walk.

The unflappable and flamboyant Mrs Morgan was bustling around the kitchen upon his return to the inn. She had piles of bacon, fried eggs, toast, and even what smelt like baked beans simmering on the stove, a full English apparently on the hob for breakfast together. It might smell divine, but he didn't know if his hunger could overwhelm his desire to avoid any of her knowing looks.

And there *would* most definitely be knowing looks. Beatrice Morgan happened to be close friends with both Francis's gran and Graham's mother. Those three could gossip with the best of them—and usually did.

If she'd seen the two of them asleep on the couch together with Zeus between them, he had no doubts it had already reached his mother's ears. He could hear her happy exclamations already.

"Oh, my son, the journalist, he's found his soul mate. Isn't it just the sweetest thing ever?"

Kill me now. I'm never going home again, sod it; Becca can ship my arse off to Antarctica for a year.

"Sit yourself down, poppet." Mrs Morgan patted one of the chairs around the small table in the kitchen, which he guessed was usually reserved for the staff as the inn had a larger dining room for guests. "Tea or coffee? Your young man will be down shortly. Did you enjoy your walk? Zeus took to you straight away, I can tell."

Poppet? Haven't been called that in ages.

He found himself guided expertly into a chair and staring down at a plate full of food before he could even begin to process all the questions that had been thrown at him. "Coffee, please. Did you say *my* young man?"

"You eat up now before it's cold."

Graham obediently began to shove a strip of bacon into his mouth in the hopes of avoiding conversation. He generally stayed away from dotty old women who always seemed to take great pleasure in managing his eating habits and romances. Rupert had always had more patience for people in general—had to, really, given his choice of career as an estate agent.

"Now, what have you two boys been up to?" She set a mug of coffee in front of him. "Enjoying the sights?"

He internally groaned, but managed to smile around his mouthful of food and struggled to get out a "Yes."

"Ahh, Mrs Morgan." BC skidded to a halt inside the kitchen, knocking over a chair in his rush. He winked cheekily at Graham, who could only stare at the shirtless man while trying not to choke on the chunk of toast stuck in his throat. "I wasn't expecting you."

"Clearly." She looked him over almost as appreciatively as Graham had. "Coffee or tea?"

"Tea."

Graham watched BC over the edge of his mug while the hulking former rugby player skulked over and slumped into the chair next to his. He appeared to be attempting to hide his upper body from view. "Feeling a tad exposed this morning, are we?"

BC elbowed him in the side, sending him to the floor with a crash. "*Shit.*"

The sheer concern in the large man's voice had Graham lifting his arm up to give him a thumbs up. He spotted Zeus out of the corner of his eye, trotting over to sniff at his shoes before starting to lift one leg. It sent him rolling quickly out of the way of any potential streams.

A roar of laughter from BC battled with the shouting and banging of the impressively loud Mrs Morgan. She chased Zeus out of the kitchen, telling him to "leave the pretty ginger lad alone." Her description served only to send a certain laughing knobhead even further into hysterics.

Graham sat up slowly, resting his arms on his bent knees. "Not sure if this is better or worse than the time my mum walked in on me with my first boyfriend."

"At least I put trousers on."

He let the words sink into his brain before joining BC in yet another outburst of mirth, which lasted longer than the first one. "Oh God, I hurt. I can't breathe. You complete plonker."

"Don't worry, Ginger Spice, I won't tell anyone how pretty you are." BC dodged the kick sent his way. "Oi!"

"Book sniffer."

CHAPTER TEN

BC

BC woke up to find himself all alone in the bed aside from Zeus, who had snuck in at some point. Graham had obviously made his escape early in the morning. BC found the sudden emptiness and quiet disappointing.

And where the bloody hell has he gone?

A quick assessment told him several important things. His sides still ached from hours of laughter. The rush of energy from days filled with good sex and adventure hadn't quite worn off yet. He also had a monstrously unhealthy hunger for chips and sausage slathered with ketchup.

The previous day had been spent trying out the last of the restaurants and bakeries on their list of best pasties in Cornwall; Graham had mainlined antacids throughout the day. It had taken the majority of the morning and afternoon.

They'd made time to visit Mawgan Porth for photos and no skinny-dipping.

The ginger journalist seemed to struggle quite a bit with indigestion. BC couldn't get a straight answer when he asked about it. Graham had simply muttered about "exotic foods and greasy chips" and moved the conversation on to something else.

After having enjoyed the last few days together, BC had hoped to have made some sort of impact on the journalist. *Why do I care?* The disappearing act told him Graham had no intention of their sleeping together evolving into anything further.

And that is that.

But why do I care?

He couldn't think about the previous night without getting hard. "Stop thinking about him, you numpty."

The minute mutt beside him gave a yip of agreement. Scolding himself failed to do a bloody thing for his morning erection. He found it impressive, given the number of pleasurable activities he and Graham had engaged in over the course of the past few days.

Sinking into the covers after setting Zeus on the floor, BC let his mind draw him to the previous night. It wasn't difficult considering the room still smelt strongly of sex, cologne, and a particular blend of honey and coffee, not a bad combination. He lost himself in images of sex with Graham. It brought him to completion almost embarrassingly quickly.

A quick bath had him right as rain, ready to get dressed for the day. Only one massive problem: what did he do now?

He opened a window to clear the room out and hopefully clear his head a bit as well.

Guests would be arriving later that afternoon to enjoy the last vestiges of Cornish winter before spring. March had crept up on him. With the distraction of a certain ginger gone, BC had to face his fate as an innkeeper—and a dog owner.

He could at least have left a note.

Deciding to stretch his legs, BC finished dressing and whistled for Zeus to follow. The dog did appear to be getting used to the idea of a new owner. He hadn't left any further passive-aggressive messes for him to deal with.

Yet.

The wind had picked up a great deal overnight, and dark clouds had filled the previously blue sky. He glared up, daring the rain to fall on him. It wouldn't be the most inspiring start to his day.

If life were a movie, BC thought perhaps the storm would leave him soaking drenched *just* in time for Graham to come running up to him with an umbrella. But life wasn't a sodding movie. Reality meant he would end up with pneumonia, no Ginger Spice, and a small, smelly, wet dog.

Standing on the beach while Zeus darted around him like a mad hare, BC couldn't help thinking a shift had happened in his mind without him realising it. Casual relationships had worked perfectly for him for so long. He'd never been interested in more, so why did he feel *sad* about Graham taking off?

Judas Priest.

He kept returning to one thing—why had Graham left

so suddenly? They'd planned on having breakfast together. What had sent him running at the break of dawn?

A text from Rupert didn't provide an answer. He mentioned his brother had driven all morning to reach Heathrow and would apparently be hopping on a flight to Finland. The estate agent wanted to know why his twin had decided to leave almost two weeks early.

How the bloody hell am I supposed to know?

Returning to the inn, BC mentally ran through his to-do list. He left Zeus and meals for the guests in Mrs Morgan's capable hands. His mind refused to focus, so clearly a chat with someone who understood would have to happen soon.

Fifty minutes later, he stood outside of Haddy's Pub in Looe. The owner of the bar, Caddock, had promised to have a drink with him. Who better to ask for advice than a confirmed bachelor who had recently married a younger man?

"He's upstairs." A woman behind the bar pointed towards a narrow staircase that led to the second floor. "I'll send up a few beers with the meat pie the chef has in the oven."

His former teammate sat behind a massive antique desk, poring over a spreadsheet filled with numbers. BC had to ignore his instinctive desire to take the mickey. He couldn't once recall seeing Caddock ever appear quite so studious in the past.

"Sit."

BC dropped into a nearby chair and waited for his friend to finish. "You sure you can count high enough to do the pub's books?"

"*Funny.*" Caddock scribbled his signature at the corner

of the document before tossing it on a stack of papers. "What brings you here?"

"Graham…."

"Oh fuck, now I owe Rupert fifty quid. *Bastard*," Caddock grumbled sharply. "I thought for sure you'd visit him, not me."

Nice.

It might've been wiser to have a chat with Francis. His rugby mates clearly couldn't resist gossiping about him behind his back and making bets. He shouldn't complain, as he'd do the same in their place.

"Well? Out with it, BC, I'm not getting any younger."

BC rolled his eyes and had to chuckle when the bartender interrupted with a tray holding the drinks and food previously mentioned. He waited until everything had gotten situated to continue. "I've no idea where to start."

"The beginning?"

"Want to wear this pie as a hat?" BC threatened.

"Not particularly."

The two shared a grin. He didn't honestly know how to ask for help. How did he find the words when so far his mind hadn't come to a conclusion on what he wanted?

Caddock leant forward in his chair, resting his elbows on the desk. "Why don't you message his editor? She'll know where to find him."

"And then?"

"If you don't know what to do then, I wouldn't bother giving her a call." He popped a chip into his mouth and took his time chewing before continuing. "You obviously enjoyed the sex. Did he make you laugh? Do you miss him?"

BC gave a helpless shrug. His immediate reaction towards wanting to find Graham continued to baffle him. "No idea."

"Maybe figure that shit out first, then?"

With Rebekah Jones's number in hand, BC decided to cut his visit short. He normally got on marvellously with Caddock, but he didn't feel up to their usual joking around.

He had a quick text conversation with Rebekah, which provided him with the next stop on the elusive wanderer's itinerary. Saariselkä, Finland. And then Palau; neither country was around the corner. She also mentioned Graham had warned he intended to be away from his laptop and mobile for the length of his visit to the Arctic Circle.

Judas Priest. Flying, almost scarier than spiders. Almost.

CHAPTER ELEVEN

GRAHAM

On a scale of one to ten, Graham's plan of avoidance had failed to the tune of negative twelve degrees Celsius. No mobile, no laptop, and no books, so plenty of time to think about why he'd scurried away from Cornwall so early in the morning. His twin had tormented him all the way to Heathrow.

The ice resort in Saariselkä should've been a dream after the heat of Australia and the dreary damp of home. *Should've.* He had always enjoyed visiting such out of the ordinary places. Why would a hotel made out of igloos be any different?

It would've been ideal except for one insignificant detail; everywhere he looked, every person seemed to take on the appearance of BC for the briefest of moments. He saw the damn man in every strange face in the distance. His neck might've suffered permanent damage from the number of double takes he'd done.

The men inevitably ended up being complete strangers. They had nothing in common with BC. Graham sought refuge in his room to avoid further humiliation.

It didn't help.

His thoughts wandered without permission to all the wonderful ways of heating one's temperature up on cold nights. All the ideas featured a particular former rugby player quite heavily, of course. He couldn't seem to escape the man even in his own mind.

As a more extreme distraction was needed, Graham threw himself into all the Arctic Circle had to offer. The magazine would cover the expenses; might as well take advantage. He had always enjoyed playing the intrepid explorer.

The first adventure hadn't been well chosen. An hour into the reindeer safari had him frozen and bored out of his mind. He would have to use a bit of creativity to make it sound enticing.

Maybe a bit unfair.

His trouble came from the beautifully serene snow-covered landscape giving him no escape from his mind. Fishing hadn't proved any better; neither had staying up late to watch the aurora borealis in the night sky. An exquisite sight, yes, but not one that made him forget the unforgettable.

Write a bloody sonnet, why don't you?

What are you running from?

His brother's words continued to roll around his brain

like marbles. Graham couldn't honestly pinpoint what had panicked him. It had all seemed so entirely domesticated at the inn in Torpoint.

They had fallen into a relaxed easiness with each other far too quickly. It had thrown Graham out of his comfort zone. He pressed his lips together in a grimace, scratching absently at the back of his neck.

What am I running away from?

The bed might have been comfortable in his ice hotel, but sleep avoided him. He had never doubted his choices before, so why start now? *Bloody Rupert and his sodding insights.* The tightness in his chest wouldn't leave no matter how much he attempted to dismiss his conflicting emotions.

On his last day in Finland, Graham decided to give snowmobiling one final try. Rebekah always wanted more photos than he sent her. He might as well use his last hours for something other than mental dithering.

Riding out into the chilly wilderness, Graham found a spot to stop and go for a walk. The snow crunched beneath his boots. He had gone far enough that the only sound came from the wind battering against him. The temperature had definitely dropped further, with the heat stripping off him with each arctic blast.

The stark winter sun glinted off the hard-packed snow. Sniffling against the cold, Graham clumsily worked his camera while combatting his chill-soaked fingers and thick gloves. His first photos were a blurry mess thanks to his lack of dexterity.

Shit.

He'd give his brother's right arm for a warm cup of tea. "What the hell am I doing out here?"

He consoled himself with the knowledge his next trip would be to Palau where warmth and jellyfish beckoned. The island would be lovely this time of year. March usually saw a dry heat, perfect for exploring all the magic of the Pacific Ocean.

He shook his head softly with a pained sigh of recognition. Rupert had been right. He was fleeing from regrets.

A lifetime ago, or so it felt, Graham had gone back and forth between the beds of two fellow students in his college. He had assumed his openness about being disinterested in monogamy meant both understood not to become attached to him. His youthful ignorance had caused him to be far more callous than intended.

When Graham had ended both dalliances upon graduation, he had been ready to move on to new adventures, both sexually and with his career. No harm had been meant, but it had been done in any case. His female lover had wished him well, happy to remain friends—she'd become his editor.

His male lover hadn't taken things quite so well. Graham discovered later that the young man had suffered from undiagnosed bipolar disorder. It had been a close thing, saving his life, keeping him from doing fatal harm to himself.

It had been a tipping point for him. He'd promised himself never to allow others to get attached to him. He was usually honest to the point of brutality when it came to his intentions in any of his flirtations.

No more breaking hearts, or so Graham had vowed. He'd felt noble about it in his twenties. Now, in his thirties, it seemed daft and self-absorbed.

Is that why I fled like a thief in the night?

They'd been sleeping soundly in bed when Graham woke up. He'd found himself intertangled with BC. It had felt domestic—good—and terrifying, so he did what came naturally and ran.

Am I ready for more?

Is that why I didn't have the discussion with him before we shagged?

CHAPTER TWELVE

BC

The initial flush of wanting to race across the world after Graham faded all too quickly. Reality hit BC hard in the guise of guests arriving. Inns tended to require someone to run them.

Mrs Morgan might be the housekeeper and cook, but he couldn't simply fob everything on her shoulders. His uncle had willed the place to him. He couldn't throw his responsibilities away to chase after a man.

Well, he could, but it would be bad form.

Only two weeks into March saw BC singing an altogether different tune. He'd discovered quite painfully that he did *not* inherit his grandmother's gift in dealing with masses of people. Screaming children and overly amorous couples eroded his patience into nothing.

Today had been the last straw, getting his bulky body

trapped in the tiny bathroom of one of the guest suites. One of the little twits had managed to break off the hot water knob. He almost wrenched his knee in his attempt to play caretaker.

Taking one look at him dripping on the stairs after making the repair, Mrs Morgan sat BC down in a chair in the kitchen. She warmed him up with a cup of tea and a plate of scones fresh from the oven. Her tutting over the state of him cheered his mood slightly.

"Why are you here, poppet? You should go after your young man." She bustled around the kitchen, making quick work of kneading dough, likely bread for later in the evening. "It's clear as day your heart has raced off after him. Why haven't you followed?"

"The inn—"

"Has stood for how many years? You think it's going to fall to pieces without you here?" She topped off his tea after he gulped down three quarters of the mug in one long drink. "You just think about it, poppet. I can handle the guests."

"I couldn't."

"Why?"

Yes, why?

The logical, business-minded, guilt-ridden side of BC's brain told him staying would be the *right* thing to do. His uncle had made the inn his responsibility. It had been his family's pride and joy for centuries. How could he leave it with the housekeeper?

His father had always told him off for pushing work off on others. He'd been accused of laziness by his trainers throughout his career. Their words still rattled around in his mind like battering rams.

"We see great potential in Boyce Brooks, but only if he learns how to push himself. He has been given every opportunity to work towards team captain and the first string of the national team. He seems content to do the bare minimum at all times. He arrives at training last and is always the first to leave. He appears to have no drive to win. The Lions cannot have a man on the pitch whose heart isn't engaged in the game."

They hadn't been wrong. His bare minimum had always been enough before. He hadn't realised his mistake until his spot on the team slipped out of his grasp; bailing on the inn at the first distraction felt like more of the same.

Judas Priest.

The whinging, even internally, had to stop before he went completely mad. He did finally have to admit to himself the debacle of his lost career was set firmly on his shoulders and no one else's. He would own his problems completely, for the first time in his life.

Good. Progress. Don't bollocks it up.

Face it, then you can move on with your head up. Isn't that what Mum always says?

"Sort yourself out, poppet. I'll have little Jackie take Zeus for a walk." Mrs Morgan had an uncanny ability to sense the depth of his thoughts. "Back in a tick."

Barely registering her exit, BC continued to ponder over his sudden paradigm shift. Wallowing in frustration had gotten him nowhere. He had to be more proactive in the course of his life.

What do I want?

Someone to manage the inn? It would be a nice place to start. He could delve into his startlingly unresolved attachment to a particular ginger after more pressing issues had been handled. He wondered if maybe his uncle had intended for the will to provide something to shake his nephew up.

Wait, someone to manage the inn?

He broke into a broad grin. "Brilliant."

"Talking to yourself?"

BC had an inspiration whack him upside the head, and he turned his most charming smile towards a suddenly suspicious Mrs Morgan. "Say the inn was yours to manage, what would you do with it?"

"Pardon?"

"If the Fisherman's Refuge were yours, how would you change it?"

She took a surreptitious sniff of his empty teacup while filling it. "Change it?"

"I'm not taking the mickey or pissed. It's a serious question."

Mrs Morgan poured herself tea and sat across from him at the sturdy, antique table in the kitchen. "I can throw together the occasional meal, but a chef wouldn't go amiss. The stairs are hard on my old legs, so maybe someone to help with cleaning. Davie never knew much about bringing in guests, not like your gran did."

"Marketing?"

"That." She nodded sagely.

She had a point, several brilliant ones. BC wondered if

it would be hard to convince her to take on a more involved role. He had no idea how to take on everything, and she'd been involved in the place since before his uncle took over.

"Ask, poppet."

"Ask?"

"I've never met a Brooks whose face didn't say everything for him." She stirred her tea absently while listening to him bungle his way through his idea. "Are you certain?"

"I...."

"Don't say yes, think about it for another day." Mrs Morgan stood and headed over to refill the kettle. "Hire locally, they'll work better for you—and me."

"Smart."

"I've got a brain under this head of grey hair." She patted his arm gently. "Now, what about your lad?"

"He's not—"

"But you'd like him to be?" She reiterated a conversation he'd had with himself. "What's the harm in trying?"

Because it's too soon.

Because I'm afraid.

Because I don't want to look like a fool.

Because. Because. Because.

How about I've managed to bollocks up everything else in my life because I'm a lazy arse who can't be bothered?

"Poppet?" Mrs Morgan tapped him on the head with a teaspoon until he opened his eyes. "You know thinking about someone and wanting to have breakfast in the morning with him doesn't mean you've gone and fallen in love. Love's a funny thing, isn't it? Never happens when it's convenient. It might surprise you with its suddenness or creep up on you slowly like a climbing vine in the garden. Enjoy it."

"But...."

She turned to stare at the window with a decidedly wistful sigh. "One day, poppet, love will have slipped through your fingers. Don't spit in Cupid's eye if you don't have to. Go, enjoy your ginger. Maybe it ends in a month. Or perhaps you find yourself falling head over trainers for him. Anything's better than moping around like a sad sack for weeks on end with no one but Zeus and an old housekeeper for company."

CHAPTER THIRTEEN

GRAHAM

Over the course of his travels, Graham had generally managed to avoid obnoxious things like common colds and flu. He'd never been prone to seasickness or overly bothered by jet lag. It made his choice of careers ideal.

So falling ill almost immediately upon arriving in Palau had put a massive damper on the entire trip. Graham languished in his bungalow on the water for two days. He *never* got sick, which made him the worst patient in the world.

He moaned, whined, and made the most unfortunate impression on the lovely woman who brought him breakfast by vomiting violently on her.

On the third day, the hotel manager had sent a doctor to him. His diagnosis of food poisoning had been pointless. Graham had in his delirium made a further nuisance of himself by attempting to go for a swim. The pint of the ocean he'd swallowed hadn't much improved his queasy stomach.

A swipe of his credit card had extended his stay by several days, since he doubted his stomach would allow him to handle a long flight to anywhere by his original check-out date. He curled up on the lounge chair on the deck to stare mournfully at the crystal-clear water. The beautiful weather mocked him.

His diet of rice biscuits and fizzy water hadn't sustained him but did keep him from fainting or ending up in the hospital. Rebekah had played mother hen over the phone, texting at least once an hour.

Rebekah: Are you dead yet? No? Good.

He'd find a way to return her kindness when his stomach stopped attempting to escape from his body via his throat.

"I am quite clearly hallucinating." Graham blinked blearily at the vaguely familiar man.

The blurry figure before him crouched down so they were on eye level. His mirage turned into a worried BC. Graham wondered if perhaps he should call the doctor again, as the food poisoning had apparently progressed into something far more dangerous.

"You're not hallucinating." BC tapped him on the head. *Bloody hell, sounds like him too.*

"Seriously, you numpty, I'm not a mirage. You're not hallucinating. I've come for a visit." BC rested a large hand against his forehead. "You sure you should be out in this sun?"

"Aren't you afraid of flying?" Graham would blame his inanity on having been sick for so long. "Are you certain you're real?"

BC paused in where he'd been dragging the large umbrella over from the table to cover Graham from the burning heat. "Quite certain."

In his travelling around the globe, Graham couldn't ever recall being this out of it, not even the one time in that one place where he'd tried the plant which may or may not have caused him to hallucinate for eight hours. *Never mind.* Dying might've been a better option, but he didn't have the energy to smother himself. He could barely keep his head up without the aid of the cushion.

He screwed his face up in a grimace to attempt to stave off yet another bout of nausea. "I'd move if I were you."

"Up you go." BC helped him shift in the lounge more comfortably. "I've ordered some ginger tea, might help your stomach."

"Ginger tea?"

"Ancient family secret." He tucked the blanket more securely around Graham, who realised he'd started to shiver again despite the heat. "You should've told someone how ill you were."

"I did." Graham closed his eyes, tilting his head to catch the warmth of the sun. "Never get sick."

The vile wanting to sick up sensation returned, and Graham found it almost impossible to get up quickly enough. BC caught him gently by the sides, avoiding touching his stomach, and carried him into the loo. He seemed completely unbothered by the unpleasant sights, sounds, and smells.

After a quick flush, BC moved over to grab a cloth and

wet it to wipe Graham's face gently. He lifted him up and returned him to his cushioned seat. The blanket went around his shaking body, helping to lull him into a drowsy state.

"Why are you here?" Graham rubbed absently at his brow, eyes glazed from exhaustion and confusion. "Seriously, you plonker, aren't you supposed to be afraid of flying?"

"You should rest."

At any other time, Graham would've had the mental strength to push for a real answer, but he could barely lift his head from the cushion. Perhaps the interrogation could wait. The sound of the waves gently lapping against the wooden supports of the deck lulled him into his first real sleep since arriving.

The sun had gone from high in the sky to low on the horizon when Graham roused from his nap. He blinked blearily before his vision cleared. Had he dreamed his visitor?

Splashing drew his attention to the right where BC sat with his legs in the water, kicking his feet. Graham spotted a mug of cooled tea on the table to his left, along with some type of sandwiches under a transparent dome. A second tray on the other table showed his mirage had taken the time to eat a late lunch or early supper.

"Going to live?" BC spoke over his shoulder.

"It was only a flesh wound." Graham winced at the crack in his voice. His throat hurt as if he'd drunk broken glass. "I'll live."

BC scanned him concernedly before returning his attention to the now setting sun. "Your colour has significantly improved. You're not as pasty as your twin anymore."

He snorted loudly in amusement. "Pasty? Rupert will no doubt appreciate your assessment of his skin."

"Good thing it's not his skin I'm interested in assessing." BC twisted his oversized body around, his tree trunk legs stretching out in front of him. "Think you can keep down food this time?"

"Why? Do you intend to spoon-feed me?" Graham curled his lips up into a half smile. He did feel better, not 100 percent, but definitely improved.

"I'll feed you something." BC moved into the bungalow and moments later he could be heard talking to room service. He returned with a fresh glass of water. "Soup and a sandwich are on their way."

"Yes, Nurse Brooks."

Managing half of the mildly spiced fish broth and rather plain cheese sandwich almost did him in; Graham didn't care to risk another bout with sickness. He allowed BC to assist him into the bath to clean up for the first time since arriving in Palau. It went a long way to lifting his spirits.

His energy levels, unfortunately, hadn't improved at all. The meal and wash tired him out. He dozed off while being towelled dry by BC, much to his frustration and the larger man's amusement.

The following morning, Graham awoke to a solid arm coiled around him. It trapped him against an equally muscled chest. BC's nose rested against his neck, each exhale tickling his soft hairs and sensitive skin.

Brightly lit numbers on the clock told him that he'd managed to sleep for over ten hours. *Good.* A tentative stretch of his body proved the long rest had done wonders for him. He might actually be able to see some of the picturesque islands he had come to explore.

Jellyfish Lake had struck his fancy in particular. It would require at least a ten-mile hike. He might have to give himself another day to recover.

Shifting under the light cotton sheet, Graham brushed against a part of his bed partner that had definitely woken up already. He couldn't stop himself from moving his arse from side to side. Maybe Nurse Brooks would want to check his temperature to ensure he didn't have a fever.

"Might want to wait until your stomach muscles aren't cramped from being sick." BC spoke with a voice gruff from sleep. It sent shivers along Graham's spine. BC's lips grazed against the side of his neck. "How about we go for a dip in the ocean before finding breakfast?"

I'd like a dip in something.

And it's not the sodding ocean.

CHAPTER FOURTEEN

BC

Forest-green eyes swept over BC when he got out of bed. He played to his audience by stretching his body to its best advantage. The movements loosened up muscles, which had tensed during the long journey to the South Pacific.

Flying had been an experience. Not bad, but not pleasant either. First class from London to Tokyo had ensured enough space for his stretched-out legs. The planes had gotten smaller with each stop of his journey. Going from the Narita International Airport to Palau in an undersized tin can hadn't done anything for his fear of flight.

He dreaded the return trip home. How did Graham travel so frequently? The getting there had been misery, but Palau had so far exceeded his limited imagining of the place.

Simply dipping his toes in the ocean while Graham

slept had been magical for him. BC wondered if maybe the wonderment of it drew in the journalist. Paradise did have a magnetic appeal to it.

"You teasing shit." Graham's glare held more pout than actual anger. "Put some sodding clothes on. You're dangling a glass of water in front of a man dying of thirst."

He paused with his boxers held loosely in his hand, reaching down to stroke his shaft, still hard from Graham's earlier encouragement. "Want a drink, Ginger Spice?"

Three steps put him near the bed and also had Graham level with his arousal. The red-haired man sat up; his fingers reached out to encircle BC's cock. His heart beat painfully in his chest when those eager eyes peered up at him, sleep-tousled hair all over the place.

Graham stroked a few times and eventually used his shaft as a handle to drag him the rest of the way to the bed. He shifted forward to sit on the edge of the mattress with BC between his legs. His tongue swiped along the head while those nimble fingers wrapped around the base.

Good morning to me.

"I'll have that drink now." Graham twirled his tongue around the length in his mouth, pulling back to motion for BC to lie on the mattress. "C'mon, then."

The frame creaked when BC launched himself onto the bed. He rested his head on his arms and lifted his hips impatiently to entice Graham, who swatted him on the upper thigh. Teasing fingers traced along the lines of his upper body, sliding through the sparse hairs covering his chest.

"Weren't you dying of thirst?" BC complained peevishly.

Remembering belatedly how ill Graham had been for the last few days, BC caught him by the shoulders to lift him up and spread him on the bed. He lined their shafts up and gently rocked forward. They both moaned, though one seemed more pained than the other.

"Stomach muscles?" BC mentally berated himself for even starting something so soon after the man had been ill repeatedly for days. He flopped on his back with a dramatic sigh. "Toast and tea?"

"Without cream."

The wry comment caught them off guard, sending them into fits of laughter. Graham rolled over on his side and groaned in pain, unable to stop his snickering. They slowly regained control only to fall apart a second time when their eyes met.

"Can't. Breathe. Hurts. Dying." Graham held his side. "You plonker."

"Me? Okay, you numpty, try to remember how to breathe while I order breakfast." BC hopped out of bed to call room service, and then dragged Graham into the bathroom with him. "Let's get you washed, you dirty lad."

Bodies slicked with soap proved too much of a temptation. Once again, their fingers showed their worth, bluntly squeezing and tugging until all too soon their release swirled down the drain. He could see from the younger man's clenched jaw that his core muscles hadn't appreciated the exertion.

They dried off and dressed quickly. BC had to dig through his hastily packed luggage to find his black swim shorts.

Swimming in the ocean ranked high on his priority list for the day.

When in Rome, and all. Or, when in Palau, swim with the fishes.

By mid-afternoon, Graham had napped off and on between brief jaunts of lazy floating in the ocean. He appeared almost completely recovered and pleased with small meals staying down. BC knew they'd be off on a hike in the morning but wanted to make the evening something special.

The candlelit dinner the concierge tried to force on him would definitely not suit. *Judas Priest.* BC wasn't about to propose to Graham. His objective revolved around getting the man naked in bed, not a glossed-up version of dinner straight from some soppy romance.

The concierge bent over backwards to offer up an impressive list of exotic options from which to choose. None fit what he wanted. He could sense their growing aggravation with him.

Staring out across the rippling sea, BC hit upon the perfect idea. He always wanted creature comforts when ill, so why not indulge Graham? It would require extra effort from all involved, but they might pull it off.

As the sun set and stars started to twinkle overhead, BC led Graham out onto a private deck set out in the water down a walkway from the bungalows. A bed of cushions covered one section, facing a large flat-screen telly. The hotel staff had set a low coffee table up in between and covered it with drinks and snacks.

Using the brilliance of streaming, BC queued up the

entire collection of *The Blackadder*, another one of their shared favourites. They settled comfortably in the cushions to watch and nosh. Graham eventually stretched out on his side to ease the pressure on his sore muscles, and rested his head on BC's thigh.

Gentle waves lapped against the edges of the platform, a sharp contrast to the bungling hilarity on the television. The breeze ruffled Graham's hair lightly. All of it faded with the fingers playing absently with the coarse hairs on his leg.

In all of his relationships, long or short, BC had struggled with intimacy. It didn't come to him naturally, not the soft, non-sexual type. With Graham, a man he'd only known intimately since last summer, the word effortless sprang to mind.

If BC had any sense, he would've dove into the ocean and swum until reaching the airport. Graham's arm dropped like a heavy chain. Soft breathing meant sleep had finally claimed him.

Running will have to wait.

Slumping into a more comfortable position, BC settled in to enjoy Rowan Atkinson at his finest. He hooked his foot around the leg of the table to drag it closer. His long arms proved handy in assuring the food and drink were reachable.

Graham awoke as the last episode ended. He twisted onto his back to stare up at BC. "Did I snore?"

"Loudly. Left a puddle of drool as well."

"Arse. I did not." Graham watched him curiously for several minutes. He averted his gaze before voicing what had been on his mind. "Why haven't you ever been in any serious relationships?"

"Why haven't you?"

"Too busy." Graham shrugged.

"Same."

Graham lifted his eyebrows only to furrow his brow shortly after. "I played with someone's heart. They didn't take it well, fell into a deep depression. Maybe my intentions weren't malicious, but I've always wondered if I'd handled things differently, less bluntly, would it have ended better."

Ahh, we're going for honesty now. Do I want to share my own secrets?

"My first serious relationship as an adult ended when my boyfriend of several years sold stories to the tabloids about me to earn himself a hefty sum of money. My parents saw photos of me starkers." BC covered his face with one hand, forcing a hard breath out. "Utter humiliation. It added the final nail in the coffin to my already failing career. I crashed as spectacularly as an Olympic diver doing a belly flop."

"So, not good then?"

"No, not good." BC grabbed a handful of the Pichi-Pichi, a local treat, addictive things. He'd already scarfed down an embarrassingly large number of the sweet, coconut-covered squares. "I never saw the point in getting in deep again. I like a laugh, good sex, nothing to risk my mum's tears again."

Graham shifted suddenly, rolling away and getting to his feet. "We should get to the bungalow. Hiking in the morning, remember?"

"Right." BC raised an eyebrow at Graham's suddenly odd behaviour. "Whatever you say, Ginger Spice."

CHAPTER FIFTEEN

GRAHAM

Waking up to find the lingering effects of his illness had faded cheered Graham up immensely. He had a slight wariness at the idea of eating. Sleep hadn't come easily to him the previous night; tossing and turning continuously kept him up long after BC had started to snore.

His thoughts swirled around the man in bed beside him. They'd admitted things to each other that neither of them had shared with anyone. BC had gone out of his way to care for him the last few days, a stark divergence from his experiences in travelling alone.

Their wake-up call came promptly at seven in the morning along with croissants and slices of mango for breakfast. A coffee later saw them suited and ready for a jaunt out to the Rock Islands and Jellyfish Lake. They'd have to take a boat out and then hike for a bit.

Absolutely worth it.

Their tour operator got them out to the many limestone islands that made up Rock Islands quickly, pointing out a few of the photo-worthy spots along the way. Graham had placed Palau on his bucket list ages ago, and his anticipation grew with each passing moment. His fingers tapped out a rhythm on his camera while he snapped quick shots.

The dirt and rock-covered path through the jungle steepened significantly away from the boat. Graham gripped the rope guide tightly in one hand; his other kept a firm hold on his camera. He couldn't bring himself to stop taking photos, not even for his own safety.

BC's strong fingers splayed across his back, offering additional stability. "Easy there, Ginger Spice. Don't go tumbling down the hill."

"Stuff it." Graham focused on not tripping head over arse to his death. He absolutely didn't lean into the hand on his back. *Okay, maybe a little.* "Plonker."

Trekking through the dense jungle, the two eventually made it to the eerily calm lake. Graham stared in awe at the greenish water filled with slow-moving orange puffs. The jellyfish reminded him a bit of rings of smoke from a pipe.

It became almost immediately apparent on entering the water that BC would *not* be enjoying this particular experience. The massive former rugby player eased himself back out of the water and onto the dock within a matter of seconds. Graham tried not to laugh with the snorkel in his mouth.

Lake water would not be sanitary.

At. All.

Jellyfish had no sense of personal space. They floated around him, all over his body. *Bizarre clouds of pulsating orange rubber.* One continued to bump repeatedly into his forehead.

Moving slowly out of a fear of being stung, even though the guide swore they wouldn't be, Graham started to use his underwater camera. He hoped the images turned out well. Showing even a part of the magical experience would make them beyond imagination.

He resurfaced after a while to find BC sitting on the edge of the dock, legs carefully pulled out of the water, watching him intently. He yanked the snorkel off his face and tossed it to the man. "Not your thing?"

"Not for all the crown jewels could you get me back in there with those creatures." BC shuddered dramatically. "They tried to smother me."

"The jellyfish?"

"Evil, conniving bastards."

"Like the spiders?" Graham asked innocently.

"Also evil, conniving bastards. Maybe it's a conspiracy." BC's eyes narrowed, staring at him pointedly.

"There's one on your shoulder." Graham almost broke a rib laughing when the large man shrieked like a small child and shot to his feet. "Might've been a leaf?"

"Pain. You. Pain." BC obsessively brushed his shoulders. "Your mother smelled suspiciously of berries—elderberries."

"I'd fart in your general direction, but I wouldn't want to harm the ecosystem." Graham hefted himself up on the dock. He couldn't recall ever enjoying a trip as much as he had this one, even with the illness. "Ready to head back to the boat?"

"More than. I'm half-starved, fear makes me hungry."

Graham rubbed at his chest, trying to alleviate slight indigestion, probably leftover from being sick. "They've got lunch for us on the boat. You up for another walk, book sniffer?"

"All right, Ginger Spice."

Halfway up the peak of the hill, Graham began to question his own ability to make it. He wondered if the illness hadn't quite finished with him yet. His stomach didn't seem upset, but the utter exhaustion that hit him out of nowhere had to be connected to it.

And the belching.

Sodding belching.

The last time Graham had burped this frequently had been when Rupert bought them several cases of fizzy drinks. They'd drunk probably twenty bottles in a day. Regret came afterwards, with them too sick to enjoy anything.

Photos, lunch, BC, it all faded away in the boat. Graham barely managed to get the backpack off before slouching into one of the seats along the side of the boat. The heat of the sun combined with the mild breeze to lull him into a fitful nap.

"C'mon, Ginger Spice." BC's voice in his ear and strong hand shaking his shoulder woke Graham up. "If you don't wake up, I'm tossing your arse in the ocean."

"How kind."

Several curses later, Graham managed to get his eyes open and his brain functioning. They'd arrived at the resort already. *Fast.* He surprisingly didn't feel the least bit hungry for having missed the meal on the boat.

Damn stomach issues.

Why'd it have to ruin his perfectly wonderful afternoon? He'd never travelled with a companion, for lack of a better term, before. He liked it more than he should.

Graham rubbed his chest absently to alleviate the building indigestion. *Bloody stomach.*

CHAPTER SIXTEEN

BC

Mysteries had never interested BC. He preferred being smacked in the face with the truth as opposed to having to decipher things for himself. Yet Graham stood before him like a pale puzzle masquerading as a travel writer.

Stood might've been a generous term. Graham had slumped into the lounge outside on the deck area of the room once again. He hadn't seemed nauseous, only tired.

Too tired.

A quiet afternoon enjoying the light winds off the ocean with an excellent novel hadn't bothered him much. BC had tea and sandwiches brought out. The redhead hadn't touched one to even nibble on it.

Their luggage had already been packed, so relaxing through the evening had been a no-brainer. While Graham dozed in and out, BC read aloud from *The Road to Mars* by Eric Lidle. *How disgustingly domesticated.* It seemed no matter how hard they tried, the two easily drifted into being a couple without actually having admitted to the connection.

The following morning, they went their separate ways, Graham off to another exotic location while BC returned to Cornwall to check on the inn. He'd promised to brave another excursion in a few months.

Or weeks. I already miss the numpty.

Judas Priest, how pathetic am I?

Mrs Morgan took one look at him when he stepped through the door and laughed. "Oh, you've gone and fallen hard, haven't you?"

"Fallen in like? Definitely. Crept up on me, like you said." BC couldn't explain it. Somewhere between the vomiting and the jellyfish, those sparkling and intelligent green eyes had drawn him deep into danger before he'd realised it. "The vines might strangle me."

She bustled him into the kitchen and quickly had a mug of tea with a scone on the side for him. "The vines may strangle you, poppet, but what a way to go."

The week went by in a blur of walking Zeus along the beach and going over business plans with Mrs Morgan. She had great ideas for how to continue to modernise. BC found himself astounded that his uncle had never considered letting the woman run the place.

She's a damn force to be reckoned with.

On the Saturday after his return to Cornwall, BC received multiple texts from Rebekah, Rupert, and Francis.

All three wanted to know if he'd heard from Graham. He had apparently gotten sick, again.

His journey to the Bigar Waterfall in Romania had been cut short. Graham had holed up in his hotel, struggling with some sort of stomach virus. It couldn't be food poisoning, obviously, not so soon after Palau. He had to have contracted some prolonged something or other in Iceland.

Right? No need to panic, you numpty.

Worrying didn't come naturally to any of the Brooks family. They never planned for things. Impulsivity ran in the blood, or so BC's mother had always claimed when poking fun at his father.

Hopping on a plane to Romania had seemed the right decision when everyone encouraged him to do so. The almost ten-hour journey went by excruciatingly slowly. He worried the entire way, imagining the worst.

Aside from being green around the gills, Graham didn't come across as anywhere near dead or dying. The ginger blinked at BC when he arrived on his hotel room doorstep with no luggage in hand and concern obvious on his face. He waved the taller man inside, rolling his eyes and groaning in exasperation.

"Becca send you? Pushy bint." Graham draped a blanket around his shoulders and dropped into an oversized armchair like a boulder off a cliff. "Or was it my interfering twin shoving his nose in this time?"

"Both, actually."

"Plonkers." Graham tugged the blanket up around his body. "It's a sodding stomach virus. What else could it be?

I'll be right as rain in no time at all. They'll feel like complete twits for panicking over nothing.

"Where you off to next?"

"London." He grimaced. "Becca refuses to book another flight for me until I've gotten the all-clear from medical. Pointless waste of time, but she never listens to me. I'm perfectly healthy."

"Aside from the vomiting?"

"Yes." Graham smiled wryly. He gave a tired sigh before resting his head against the edge of the chair. "If I fly like this, I'll wind up in some sort of quarantine."

"No more movies while you're delirious." BC had initially felt relieved to see the younger man cracking jokes. It faded with how pale and drawn his face appeared in the dimly lit room. He'd have to open the curtains later to get a clearer view. "We'll fly out together in a day or two when you can walk a few feet without sicking up."

"Not necessary."

"I want to do it." BC waved off the feeble attempt to chase him off. "Who else could carry you through the airport in your weakened state? My bulk must be useful for something. I can heft you on my shoulder."

"Stupid arse." Graham flung a spare cushion at him. They both watched it sail over his head and knock a vase off the side table to crash to the floor in several pieces. "Shit."

"They'll bill you."

"It's a pity I won't even have a good story to go with how it happened," Graham grumbled mournfully. "I'll make something up."

They lapsed into silence. BC pondered his lack of luggage. Probably should've thrown something together, even if it were only a change of pants and a toothbrush. He didn't want to think of the state his clothes would be in within a few days of travelling.

"Becca texted me to say she overnighted supplies. You'll have pants in the morning." Graham interrupted his thoughts, reading his mind—or perhaps the frown on his face. "How on earth did you forget to pack?"

"Impulse, thy name is BC." He hadn't thought much beyond getting to Romania to see Graham. "How'd she know my size?"

"Never ask how Becca knows anything. You'll only terrify yourself." Graham rose slowly out of the chair, blanket slung across his body. "Are you hungry?"

"Starved."

Graham grabbed a folder from a nearby drawer and tossed it to him. "Nothing smelly—or fishy."

"Smelly?"

"Would you *like* me to vomit on you?"

"Wouldn't be the first time you've done it." And it wouldn't, they'd experienced that particularly joyous adventure in Palau.

"Plonker." Graham crawled into the bed and dragged the blanket over his head. "Maybe you should eat out. I wouldn't want to put you off by a sudden bout of sickness."

"How kind."

"*Plonker*," Graham muttered drowsily.

"So you've said, repeatedly."

When his retort received no response, BC glanced up from the room service menu to find Graham had dozed off. *Typical.* He settled on ordering a simple sandwich with tea. Might as well nosh on a late lunch while the poor bastard rested.

Graham slept. And slept. When the man wasn't resting, he spent his time bent over the toilet. The hotel staff kindly brought up clean sheets and towels. They opened the windows to allow fresh air to circulate; it helped a bit.

How could it be food poisoning? Vomiting didn't always mean a deathly illness. Graham appeared perfectly fine, outside of the getting sick.

Bored out of his mind, BC started to search through Google for possible answers. A terrible idea, since not even ten minutes in he reached the conclusion that they both had days to live. He clearly had some form of flesh-eating bacteria on his neck.

Oh God. I'm dying.

Pull yourself together, you idiotic arse. It's where you cut yourself this morning.

He spent an uncomfortable night on the couch across from the bed. A knock on the door at seven in the morning brought a bag of clothes, plane tickets, and breakfast. Becca had planned for everything; the overnighted parcel included two novels, condoms, lube, and toiletries.

Noshing on one of the plain croissants brought up for breakfast, BC started reading *Mrs Fry's Diary* by Stephen Fry. He'd chuckled into his coffee by the first page. His laughter grew with each turned page, eventually waking up a groggy Graham.

Over a plate of the croissants and milky tea, they traded off reading out one chapter after the other. Time well spent. BC had never read with someone; it seemed almost a date from a past century, and soppy, completely over-the-top romantic nonsense.

The plain breakfast didn't immediately upset Graham's sensitive tummy. He still curled up in the chair, complaining not long after of indigestion. *Indigestion? From half a croissant and a third of a cup of barely flavoured water?* Neither of them needed to say how strange it sounded.

The tickets from Graham's editor had been booked for the following afternoon. BC didn't know how the exhausted man would handle the various hops from car to train to plane required to get them on British soil once again.

I could always toss him over my shoulder to carry him.

"Whatever you're thinking, the answer is no." Graham glared knowingly at him. "You've got the same gleam in your eye that Rupert gets when he's about to do something to annoy me."

"Me? Annoy you? Would I be awful enough to do that when you're on your deathbed?" BC demurred theatrically. "More tea?"

The grimace sent his way answered the teasing question. Over the morning, they made it through half of the book. Graham managed not to sick up again, but only by the skin of his teeth, if the continued paleness were any indication.

A skipped lunch had BC's concerns skyrocketing, though Graham insisted it meant nothing. His normally made-of-steel stomach had simply reached the point of oversaturation. He'd be fine.

By evening, the missed meals continued to stack up. Toast had been snubbed, and so had the simple broth brought up from the kitchen. Everything had set Graham's stomach to churning.

"Are you preggers?" BC asked absently. He'd eaten his own dinner quickly outside in the hallway. "It might explain your sensitive tummy. Immaculate conception?"

"I'm not up the duff, you idiotic wanker." Graham casually flipped him off. "Any other theories you want to share?"

"An ulcer?" BC rattled off several of the various diseases and illnesses found in his earlier research. Graham shook his head to each one. "It might not be food or a simple virus."

"Don't be so damned morose. It's nothing to stress over." Graham continued to ignore any suggestions of a potentially serious problem. "Don't play doctor because you've looked on the Internet. It's dangerous. You'll convince yourself we're both dying if you're not careful."

CHAPTER SEVENTEEN

GRAHAM

Graham had tried to convince himself, his family, friends, and his doctor that his continued illness came from travelling too much. No one wanted to take his word for it. His general practitioner had, after seeing him twice, immediately made an urgent referral to a specialist in Plymouth.

Genevieve Williams, his new doctor, was a lovely woman who reminded him greatly of his editor, Rebekah, and not only because of their similarities in looks. She hadn't listened to any of his attempts to obfuscate. He'd had blood tests done along with having an endoscopy scheduled.

The days went by so slowly. Everyone tried to distract him while they waited to hear from the doctor. Graham could admit, at least to himself, that he had withdrawn from them all to attempt to wrap his mind around the terrifying possibilities on his own.

And so, on a beautiful late April morning, Graham sat in a chilly office with his doctor. She had the worst poker face of anyone he'd ever met. He could win a fortune off her at cards.

"What is it?" He wanted facts, not useless platitudes like the ones on the posters that lined the hallways outside. "Is it cancer? Am I dying? How long do I have?"

"Breathe, Graham, please don't panic." Genevieve stretched a tawny-coloured arm across her desk to hold his hand, which he was ashamed to find trembling. "It is stomach cancer—likely stage one, possibly stage two. We're going to need more tests to be certain. You're one of the lucky ones. We've found it far early. Many don't come in until it's progressed to stage three. Your family did the right thing in pressing you into getting checked out."

Lucky ones? I don't sodding feel lucky.

He decided not to be rude to the woman who could save his life. "Now what?"

"More tests." She smiled prettily when he groaned. "Only a few more to confirm the size and exact location. I have hopes we'll be able to surgically remove only part of the lining of your stomach. I'll know more after I can look at all the results."

"Chemotherapy?"

"Possibly." Genevieve squeezed his hand sympathetically. "More than likely, yes, you will go through it both before and after surgery. You won't be alone. The odds of survival are in your favour, at this stage. More than 80 percent chance of living for five years or more according to our statistics. You might be sick—weak—for a while, but I believe you'll make a strong recovery."

"You promise?" Graham felt too shell-shocked to fully process the life altering news. *Why didn't I say yes to BC's offer to be here with me? I'm so sodding stupid.* He glanced up to find the doctor's concerned eyes watching him. "Don't worry. I know you can't make promises. It *is* cancer, after all, even if it's an early stage of it."

Cancer.

"We'll do everything possible to help you through this." She pulled her hand away and turned towards her computer. "I'll schedule your testing for next week and have a plan for the chemotherapy to go over with you then. You'll want to talk with family and friends."

"Why?"

Her eyes softened at the faint tremble he couldn't keep out of his voice. "In my experience, the support of loved ones often makes an immense difference in recovery. It isn't weakness to want their help. Trust me when I say you will want them in this battle with you. No one should be in the cancer trenches on their own, Graham."

"Fine, fine." Graham couldn't process anything further; the doctor could clearly see it. She handed him a folder with pamphlets on treatments, a schedule, and other information before walking him to the door. He barely managed a begrudging, "Thank you."

Thank you? Go fucking suck eggs, more like.

The absurdity of offering gratitude for the gut-wrenching news would've made him laugh any other time, but the massive lump stuck in his throat wouldn't allow it. He strode quickly towards his borrowed car to gain some semblance of privacy.

I won't sob. I won't. It'll be fine. I'll be fine. I'm not going to die. I'm not— Shit.

He sat in the Porsche, borrowed from his sister-in-law for a night, for two hours. His fingers refused to turn the key in the ignition. His brain couldn't cope with the news; he couldn't handle it.

How can I— How do I— Oh, God, I have cancer. I'm too young to die. And how absurdly selfish am I when so many others are struggling with this shit like me. Why should I be different?

The thoughts raced faster than Graham could catch them. One overwhelming thing stuck with him, though—the fear of it. He could admit in the lonely silence of the sports car how utterly terrifying the news was.

"Ginger Spice?"

Graham hadn't heard the knocks or the door open, but he realised with a double take that BC had squashed his massive frame into the Porsche. "Where the bloody hell did you spring up from?"

BC had the pamphlets in his hand. His dark blue eyes held the horrified dread that Graham felt in the pit of his soul. "Cancer?"

"Most likely." He couldn't quite manage a simple yes. It seemed far too final. "More tests, some…. I can't… don't know. *Shit.*"

The former rugby player got out of the Porsche, walked around to lift Graham out of the driver side, and gently guided him into the passenger seat instead. BC got behind the wheel and fussed with his mobile for several minutes. He eventually started the car and reversed out of the parking space.

"Where are we going?"

"Read those papers." BC nodded towards everything Genevieve had given him. "It's going to take an hour or more to get there."

"Fowey?" Graham groaned.

"No, we're not going to see your parents, or Rupert either." BC winked at him. "You're right about the general direction, though."

"Shit."

That meant family, even if they went to Torpoint instead of Fowey or Looe. Rupert would call their parents; he'd call Francis, who would bring his husband. Everyone and their gran would know about the Cancer, capital letter required.

BC drove them straight to his family inn. Mrs Morgan had a plate of fresh-baked saffron buns along with brandy-laced tea ready for them. She hugged him hard before disappearing into the kitchen.

"You told her?"

"No, actually. Maybe it's your red eyes or the medical leaflets in your hands?" BC snatched up one of the buns to bite into it hungrily. "Sit. Eat. Drink."

Graham sank gratefully into one of the comfortable chairs around the fireplace in the living room. "I thought I'd be mobbed by everyone immediately upon arrival."

"Tomorrow." BC inhaled the roll and reached for another one. "Didn't think you were quite ready for everyone's sympathy to be dumped on you like a bucket of cold water."

Graham wasn't ready, might not ever be. "Thanks."

"Want to talk about it?" BC grinned when Graham yanked the plate of buns out of his reach. "What? Driving makes me hungry."

"How'd you get to Plymouth? I didn't see your vehicle."

"Train and taxi."

"Becca called you?"

"She does go out of her way to ensure you've got whatever you need. I'd be jealous if I didn't know you preferred blokes and she didn't." BC gulped down some tea only to choke and cough seconds later. "Judas Priest. She dumped half a bottle of brandy in this tea."

"Good. I'm going to need it." Graham stared unseeing into the teacup, not truly hungry or thirsty. Given the diet the doctor had mentioned, it might be the last brandy and regular food he would have for a while. He worried trying to swallow would cause his throat to seize up. "I have cancer. I. Have. Cancer."

BC dragged his chair effortlessly around the table to sit in front of him with their knees touching. He rested his large hands on Graham's legs. "You do. It's shit. Hate cancer, not fair anyone should have the cursed disease. You're not alone, Ginger Spice. I'll be here, whatever you need."

"Cancer. I have cancer." Graham shook his head in the hopes it would restart his brain. It didn't. He couldn't seem to stop repeating himself. "Sodding cancer."

"Sod cancer." BC tapped his fingers against the side of his knee. "How do you feel about *Lord of the Rings*?"

"Pardon?"

"We're going to want plenty of books to read." BC rattled off the titles of several novels. "It'll keep your mind off things."

"Off cancer?" Graham didn't think anything could make him forget. "Not even remotely possible."

"Oi. We're Brits, keep that upper lip *up*."

"Careful, you're going to start to sound like my nan in a minute." He tried some of the tea, forcing himself not to gag on it. "Let me be for now, BC. I'm struggling to take this news on the chin."

"All right, Ginger Spice."

CHAPTER EIGHTEEN

BC

Cancer.

BC had never hated a word. Disliked some, avoided using others, but never loathed one quite so much as cancer. He hadn't known his heart could muster so much angry passion. A night of uneasy sleep hadn't helped things sink in any further or tamed down his emotions one jot.

All reservations at the Fisherman's Refuge had been cancelled. Mrs Morgan had wisely suggested temporarily closing their doors, at least for a few months. Family and friends would inevitably descend on them; no point in having a slew of strangers traipsing around them. Their bottom line would take a slight hit but nothing earth-shattering.

Despite all the empty rooms, Graham had sat by the fireplace in the sitting area off the dining room. He constantly shivered even with the blanket and heat from the flames. Mrs Morgan had brought plenty of tea, exchanging the cool and untouched cup with a fresh one periodically on the off-chance he'd drink some.

He didn't.

The hordes would descend on them within the next few hours. BC could tell from the set of Graham's shoulders how uneasy it made him. Everyone wanted answers on what the results had been at the doctor.

I couldn't actually say, "Oh, he's got sodding cancer" over the phone, could I?

For the first time since moving to Cornwall, BC appreciated Zeus. The obnoxious Yorkie hadn't moved off Graham's lap once. He allowed the man to simply pet him and both ignored all attempts at conversation.

"Graham?" BC crouched in front of the chair, not taking the glare from either man or beast personally. "Rupert will be here first. I'm honestly shocked he's not here already. You should have some toast or something."

"How?"

"One bite at a time?" BC grinned when Graham managed a slightly weepy-sounding chuckle. "It's the good bread, from the new bakery in the village. I've had half a loaf of it myself."

"Greedy arse." Graham gently placed Zeus on the floor and got to his feet. He placed a hand on BC's shoulder where he knelt. "I can travel the world, but I don't know if I can beat this—not on my own."

"Who says you would be left on your own for even a

second of this fight?" Francis took the words right out of BC's mouth. The slim man walked towards them with his faithful service dog, Sherlock, at his side. His husband followed close behind him. "Whatever this dreadful news is, we wouldn't ever allow you to play the lone wolf."

BC shook hands with both men, then left them with Graham to step out to speak with Mrs Morgan. She promised to set up a buffet lunch for anyone who might be hungry. As Caddock, Rupert, and he regularly ate like starved animals, it was a stroke of genius from the woman.

The sound of a vehicle pulling up outside drew BC's attention. He found Rupert and Joanne hesitating by the front steps. The man who usually met everything with a laugh— even breaking his leg in a game hadn't soured him—appeared grim enough to seem like he might never smile again.

"How bad is it?" Rupert covered the small distance between them, taking the three steps in one bound. "Shot of whisky bad? Or the whole bloody bottle?"

BC met the man's eyes, so identical to his twin's that it took his breath away. "Bought several bottles. I'm sure we'll manage to work our way through at least four of them by the end of the day."

"God help me." Rupert reached out blindly to clutch at his wife's hand. "God help us."

"Hope she's listening." Becca slammed the door of her Mini and jogged over to them with her wild, curly black hair flying all over the place. "We'll prop him up until everything is fine again."

"Will it be fine again?" Rupert's smile was strained

at best. "What the devil's wrong with him anyway? You haven't said."

Texting the details of Graham's condition hadn't seemed the right idea. BC hadn't believed it was his place to tell the family. But now, faced with the three hovering around him, he managed to spit it out, one simple word—cancer.

The thought occurred to BC when Rupert dropped to his knees like a lead balloon that perhaps blurting out a single word might not have given them enough information. He could've couched the news better. Becca stormed away from the inn, cursing furiously and struggling to light her cigarette, leaving him to help the man up to his feet.

"He's not— The doctor said— I'll go check on Becca." BC didn't get any sort of response from the silent couple clinging to one another. They didn't seem to even register his presence. "Right, I'll talk to her, and you two sort yourselves out."

Boyce Brooks, you're a knobheaded, bumbling fool. Judas Priest. You could've told them that he's got great chances. Shit.

Even with his long legs, BC had to speed up to catch up to Becca. The editor ranted angrily to herself in French, likely a credit to her mother, and waved her cigarette around viciously. He had to dodge to avoid catching the burning ashes on his arm.

"Oh, *merde*, I'm so sorry." She brushed her fingers against his shirt as if to ensure no damage had been done. "Don't tell Graham. He's always telling me to quit—says I'll get cancer and—"

"Yes, quite." BC didn't know her well enough to offer comfort. He stood, instead, and allowed her to curse herself, cancer, and Graham until her cigarette had gone out. "I've got whisky inside."

The four gathered together by the front door. BC didn't think any of them were quite ready to face Graham with cheerful resolve. He wasn't sure the man would want feigned positivity in any case.

Mrs Morgan poked her head out the door, took one look at their weepy faces, and obviously decided an intervention would be required. She herded them all inside the inn towards the sitting area. "Make yourself at home, poppets. I'll have tea sorted in a twinkling."

"I'll help," Joanne offered after giving her husband and his twin one last squeeze of a hug. She followed the former housekeeper with Zeus darting between their feet. "Oh, isn't he darling?"

"Bugger. She'll want one of those next." Rupert grimaced in distaste at the tiny dog. His glare shifted to BC quickly. "I'm blaming you for this."

"Yeah, yeah, Ginger squared." BC didn't have the ability to force the teasing beyond what he'd already said. He watched Graham soldier through the hugs, tears, and fears of his family and friends. None of them had noticed his obvious discomfort. His instincts about the writer not being ready to deal with others bore fruit in front of him. "I don't know about all of you, but I could use something stronger than tea."

Aside from Francis who didn't drink, they all readily accepted splashes of whisky in their tea, more than a splash in some cases. All the lovely food Mrs Morgan had put together didn't seem nearly as appetising after Graham had shared the details of his visit to the oncologist. Surgery and chemotherapy were words guaranteed to sober the mood of anyone, even the perpetual jokester, Rupert.

"Fuck." Caddock's forcefully whispered oath echoed the sentiments of everyone in the room. He had his arms tightly wrapped around his husband. "What can we do?"

"Don't smother me," Graham begged hoarsely. "I'll be fine. Doctor said not to worry, so let's not fall to pieces like a bunch of ninnies."

Leaving the others to discuss how to break the news to Mr and Mrs Hodson, BC strode through the inn and out the rear exit. He stood on the bluff, allowing the sea breeze to wash over him. *Fine? I doubt those were her exact words.* Surgery and chemo didn't quite sound okay to him.

He heard footsteps and glanced over his shoulder to find Caddock walking up towards him. "Where's the little devil?"

"With his grandparents."

BC didn't care much for children, but Caddock's young nephew could charm just about anyone. "Life's thrown some curves our way, hasn't it?"

"Red suits you, BC." Caddock clapped him on the shoulder much as he used to do after a good try during a rugby match. "I get half the credit for helping you find him, since I invited you to the wedding."

"You always were a greedy bastard when it came to things to brag about." BC couldn't muster a grin for his old friend. "He's afraid. So am I."

"We all are."

"You're probably right." BC gave a half-hearted shrug.

"How long did we play together? I'm always right." Caddock puffed out his chest and winked at him.

"Smug bastard." BC elbowed his friend in the side. "I can think of a ton of occasions when you most definitely weren't right. How's married life treating you?"

"Brilliant." Caddock grinned soppily at him while rubbing his ribs. "Best idea I've ever had."

They stayed shoulder to shoulder watching the waves crashing on the rocky shore below. BC couldn't help seeing the similarities between them. Both with failed rugby careers, both moved to Cornwall, and both found love in the Cornish countryside. The main difference between them came from Caddock having his happy-ever-after, where he might lose his potential one to cancer.

The pull of his husband eventually proved too much for Caddock, who returned to the house. BC stayed on the edge of the cliff, metaphorically and literally. Mermaids could've come up out of the ocean for all the attention he was paying to the scene before him.

Echoes of the waves on the beach usually soothed him. BC heard none of it. His mind refused to let go of his worry, no matter how he tried to consider the matter logically.

"Mrs Morgan has the buffet set up." Graham broke him out of his thoughts. He had the feeling he'd stood outside longer than anticipated. "Next time you invite all the interfering wankers in my life to harass me, you could have the decency to keep me company."

"Poor Ginger Spice." BC chuckled deeply. "Want me to rescue you? Didn't think damsels in distress was your kink."

"Oi!" He whacked BC on the arm. "Don't be an arse."

"C'mon, then, I'll slay the dragons for you." He threw an arm around the man's shoulders. "Zeus'll help save you."

"Plonker."

CHAPTER NINETEEN

GRAHAM

By the end of May, Graham had his official diagnosis of stage one gastric adenocarcinoma plus a plan of action: chemotherapy before surgery to remove the cancer, which would be followed by additional rounds of the chemo. He'd be in the hospital in June to have the affected parts of his stomach lining removed. If he'd had the energy to be afraid, it would've terrified him.

His oncologist had introduced him to Freddie Whittle, who would coordinate all of his appointments and doctors. Graham had never imagined his life would slow to a crawl while a specialist cancer nurse moved him around like a chess piece. The chemo made him too tired to care.

After Rupert had told their parents, his mum wanted him to move back home with them. He'd tried it for a week, less than, really. Five days had him climbing the walls while his mother coddled him to death and his dad told him to buck up and take it like a man. What did that even mean?

Helpful, Dad. And the cabbage, the sodding cabbage.

His mum had read somewhere it could help reduce cancer cells. She'd practically force-fed him buckets of the stuff as soup. He'd had enough of it to last him a lifetime.

One call had BC driving to the rescue. Graham found himself comfortably ensconced in one of the first-floor rooms at the inn. It had been fixed up especially for him.

Working with information from Freddie and Genevieve, BC, along with Francis, Caddock, and Rupert, with Mrs Morgan directing them, had created the perfect recovery space for him. With an en-suite and a private door that led outside, Graham had everything at his fingertips. It had a flat-screen telly, books, and his laptop. Becca had brought in poster-sized photos from his travels to line the walls.

Unbeknownst to him, Mrs Morgan had coordinated with the nutritionist assigned to him by Genevieve. She'd promised him not a drop of cabbage soup would come out of her kitchen. The list of approved foods was focused on ensuring his meals helped, not hurt his chances of a full recovery.

"Mum's pouting but Dad's pleased to have his comfy chair back." Rupert flopped on the king-sized bed next to him. His twin had been spending quite a bit of time with him since finding out. "She sent cabbage soup. Mrs Morgan donated it to one of the local farmers for his pigs."

"If I smell cabbage one more time...." Graham grimaced

in complete disgust. "My appetite's shit as it is. Mum didn't help."

"It's good for you." Rupert snickered at him. "Mrs Morgan promised not to try soups of any kind so as not to traumatise you further."

"Don't you have houses to sell or a wife to chat up?" Graham couldn't remember his brother ever being so stationary. He might've been the wanderer of the family, but his elder twin had ants in his pants in his own way. "Joanne must be celebrating having the house to herself so much lately."

"I worry." Rupert played with the frayed edges of the quilt that covered his legs. "What would I do without my little brother?"

"Little? By what? Five whole minutes?"

"I learnt a lot in those extra minutes." Rupert kept his gaze firmly focused on his hands, but Graham could still make out tears forming at the corners of his eyes. "I don't mind so much when you leave me behind to travel, but this insidious disease…. I won't be the only twin standing. You hear me? I won't. You'll fucking recover because I can't deal with a world without you in it. Someone has to be the uglier version of me."

"Rupert." Graham had tried so hard not to break down, and succeeded well up to this point. The hitch in his brother's voice broke the stopper on his own emotions. He yanked the blanket over his head to hide from his twin—and himself. "Shit."

His older brother's arms went around him, blanket

and all. "You'll be okay, Grimmie."

Grimmie?

Graham choked on a laugh and tears at the old nickname. They'd had such trouble with each other's names as toddlers. "Okay, Rup-Rup."

"Rup-Rup?"

He yanked the quilt off his head to find a smirking BC watching from the doorway. "No comments from the book sniffer."

Rupert's gaze flicked between the two of them. "I'm quite certain I don't want to know where you came up with that moniker."

"Mind out of the gutter, Rup-Rup." BC's eyes narrowed on the man, though he winked at Graham. "Mrs Morgan thinks you should attempt lunch out on the picnic table in the back garden. It's, and I quote, 'too lovely for your ginger poppet to stay inside.' So? Shall we?"

"I better make sure my office hasn't collapsed into chaos." Rupert kissed the top of his brother's head and darted out of the room with the parting shot, "No sniffing books or anything else."

"He kissed my head." Graham stared bewildered at the empty doorway. He ran his fingers through his hair only to come out with a clump of it for his trouble. "Oh."

Oh.

Everyone had warned him this might happen. Graham had known and tried to prepare himself for the first time; said it wouldn't bother him if it did happen. He'd been naïve.

Why should it? Graham had never been overly vain

about his appearance. A little lack of hair wouldn't be the end of the world. Yet, now faced with the reality of it, it did bother him.

Staring down at the reddish-blond hair in his hand, Graham found it difficult to breathe all of a sudden. BC quickly strode across the room to sit on the edge of the bed. He reached out to take the strands of hair out of shaking fingers.

Closing his hand around the red wisps, BC shoved them into his pocket. Graham couldn't shake himself out of the shock. He didn't react when strong fingers threaded with his own.

"I could pretend." Graham found a hidden masochistic streak in his personality. He reached up with his free hand to feather his fingers through his hair again, losing even more. "This is fucking real—the chemo pills and the surgery. I've got cancer."

"Shave it." BC tilted his own head down. "Works for me. We'll have a matching set."

"Idiot." He chuckled despite the fear gnawing away inside his chest. "You're not shaving my head. We're not in a soppy romance novel, are we?"

"Already taken care of the problem." BC waved off his half-hearted teasing. "Remember Jack Sasaki—the barber from Fowey? He's stopping by tomorrow to give you a little snip-snip. Francis set it up for you. He's got a friend, Vi, who runs some sort of soap shop. She's made some sensitive skin stuff for you, since Freddie mentioned your skin might suffer from the treatment."

"BC." Graham found himself continually moved by the

lengths to which the man went to help ease his pains and offer comfort where possible. "Thank you, for all of this."

"Let's have some lunch." BC helped him outside. "We've got popsicles as well, in case your mouth starts to hurt. Freddie mentioned we should stock up on them."

The luncheon set out on the table should've been mouth-wateringly appetising: grilled chicken sandwiches with lightly roasted vegetables, all doctor-approved and good for him. Graham cursed his non-existent appetite. He didn't do much more than nibble at the food like a bunny with a carrot.

"Have you had your pills for the day?" BC tended to remember them more often than Graham. "All of them?"

He eyeballed the chips on BC's plate morosely. He wanted them—craved them, even. "I could—"

"Not even one." He shifted the plate out of reach. "No grease. Pretty sure the vinegar and the salt wouldn't do your tummy much good either."

The very idea of oil sent his stomach churning immediately. He pressed his lips tightly together and turned his head to allow the breeze to waft across his face. The warm sun and cool ocean air brought him out of the sudden bout of nausea.

BC inhaled the last bits of his meal before grabbing their plates. "Back in a tick."

While his lunch companion ducked into the inn, Graham decided to try a bit of exercise. He struggled to get up to the top of the bluff. His legs shook with the effort of moving up the small incline.

A month or two ago, Graham would've easily hiked for miles and enjoyed it immensely. The chemotherapy had sapped him of his usual vigour. He could barely manage to keep on his feet; he'd locked his knees to stop from hitting the ground.

"Easy, Ginger Spice." BC jogged up behind him. His muscular arms wound around his waist to offer support. "Up here, I can understand why my family bought this parcel of land. What's got your mind so occupied?"

"Writing." Graham allowed his head to drop back against his chest. No one was around to see his weakness. "How does a travel writer work without going anywhere?"

"More stories on Cornwall then?"

He shook his head minutely. "I've exhausted my interest in the topic. Becca wants me to write about the whole cancer situation. The truth about it, not the prettified telly version of it."

"And? Don't you want to do it?"

"Don't know." He shrugged.

The treatment hadn't only sapped his energy. Graham struggled to keep his attention on simple things like reading the paper. How could he put some sort of intelligent column together? It would be a strain, a fact that made him so exhaustingly angry he could spit nails.

"You're getting cold again." BC rested his hands on Graham's shoulders, which had started to tremble. He guided him carefully down the hill to the inn and brought him to the fireplace in the library. "Shall we finish up *Good Omens*?"

Reading together had become a daily occurrence.

BC usually got through several chapters in one sitting. Graham frequently dozed off in the middle, not that the man complained.

Graham's mind kept drifting to the issue of hair loss. He couldn't help but wonder if his entire body would be affected. "Think I'll lose my pubes?"

BC snorted the tea he'd been drinking through his nose, barking out a laugh and coughing hoarsely as a result. "What?"

"Freddie said I could potentially lose all of my hair. What about my pubes?" Graham smirked while BC mopped up his tea. "Maybe I should write about that sort of thing."

"Losing pubic hair?"

"What? It happens. Doc said it did. It's even in those glossy pamphlets she gave me." Graham had found it amusing and horrifying at the time. "People shouldn't be ashamed to talk about this shit."

"No, they shouldn't." BC watched him over the top of the book. "Think Jack would shave down there as well?"

"I'll give you fifty quid to ask him." Graham brought a hand to rub at his eyebrows. "All my hair could go—eyebrows, everything."

"Yes, so I gathered."

"Think they make wigs for your pubes?"

"No, no I don't." BC met his eyes briefly, all it took to have them both snickering. "Ask Genevieve."

"Not a chance in hell."

CHAPTER TWENTY

BC

Finding the right shop in Plymouth had been an adventure, particularly with Caddock attempting to direct him from the GPS on his mobile. The man might be brilliant on the pitch and at running a pub, but he had no sense of direction. They'd ended up halfway across the city before realising they'd gone the wrong way.

As Caddock had the largest and most comfortable vehicle out of all of their friends, he had volunteered to drive them all up to Plymouth for Graham's weekly check-up. It would be the last one prior to his surgery. Francis had gone to the clinic with Graham while BC had been left with his idiotic husband.

They'd been hunting for a shop with winter wear for Graham all morning. Even given the summer month, the man had been struggling to keep his head and hands warm. They had to find a solution for him.

Grumbling like grumpy old men at each other, BC lambasted his former teammate's intelligence while Caddock complained about his driving. They had to laugh at the ridiculousness of it when they realised the store was right in front of them. It had only taken them going around in circles to find the blasted place.

"How about this one?"

"Unless Graham has suddenly morphed into a five-year-old girl, I don't believe he'll be wanting a pink hat with a pink pig in a dress on it." BC flung a matching pair of pink mittens at the idiot. "Why couldn't Francis have come shopping with me? You're a useless bastard. Put the damn bear hat down, I don't care if it's fleece and warm. *Numpty.*"

"Maybe we should stop looking in the kids' section?"

"Good idea."

Deciding to disregard anything Caddock brought to him, BC pulled together an excellent collection of knit hats and gloves. He hoped they would cheer Graham up a bit. He'd been dreading this last trip to the doctor for obvious reasons.

Most of the items had been pulled out of a back room as winter wear wasn't exactly a typical summertime purchase. Once explanations had been given as to why they wanted them, the staff at the shop had been more than willing to hunt out stock from the previous year. Most of the hats they purchased were beanies of various colours and knits; hopefully at least one of them would be comfortable and warm enough to serve their purpose.

Six hours later, Graham had a burgundy beanie with bear ears on his head. It had been the one silly purchase of the morning. BC should've known his wanderer would love it best. They kept the *regular*-looking hats for trips beyond the Fisherman's Refuge.

One glove had been sacrificed to a god. Zeus had snatched it straight from the shopping bag. They hadn't been quick enough to stop the mini menace. The Yorkie had dragged it underneath a sofa and snarled at anyone who tried to take it off him.

Idiotic creature.

Aside from losing his hair, Graham's body suffered from other side effects. His skin grew paler, and his nails were brittle. They'd gotten lotion to help with his dry and irritated skin.

"What's the matter?" BC dropped into his usual seat in the library, weary from a long day out. He'd noticed Graham growing quieter and more withdrawn as the evening progressed. "Did Genevieve have bad news for you?"

"No, not really." He studied the book in his hands, a collection of Sherlock Holmes tales. They'd finished their last novel the night before last, so it was time to move on to another one. His fingers traced the well-worn edges of the paperback. "My immune system might never fully recover. What if I can never travel again? I'd be alive, but not able to do what makes me feel like I'm doing more than merely surviving. It's such complete shit. I hate this—this weakness."

"You'll—"

"No pointless platitudes, not tonight, I'm begging you."

Graham snapped the book shut sharply, cutting him off midsentence. "I'm so sodding tired of being stuck in one place unless I'm being carted off to the doctor. It's been over four weeks, and I'm already going mad with it. How will I ever manage months and months of it? Or what if I can never travel? I'll go bonkers."

How did one respond to hopelessness? BC didn't take the desire to leave personally. For someone who thrived on adventure and exploration, he could well imagine how trapped the other man must be feeling in this situation.

Nothing anyone could do would make it better. His dad had always claimed one couldn't move beyond something awful without getting all the sorrows and emotions out first. It hurt to not be able to do anything more than sit quietly while Graham vented his fears and frustrations.

"I'm sorry. I must sound like an ungrateful arse and whiny little shit." Graham rubbed his eyes tiredly. "The hats are brilliant. Head's warm for the first time in ages."

"Think you've earned the right to whinge."

Graham grinned wryly at him. "You didn't disagree, though, did you? *Plonker.*"

"Want me to lie?"

"Yes, yes I do."

"All right then, you're a model of perfect manners and grace." BC caught the hat thrown at him easily. He shoved it on his own head. "Keeping it, spoils of war. Oh, it is all lovely and warm."

Graham's burst of laughter didn't last long. His eyes dimmed while shifting to stare into the fire. "Genevieve believes the surgery should get all of the bad tissue. It could come back, though, often does. What would you do if you might only have five years to live?"

"Whatever makes me happy and sod anyone who thinks it's selfish. If I had a time limit on my life, I'd make sure I had plenty of good laughs before I died." BC had thought about it quite a bit ever since the cancer diagnosis. "How about you? What would you do?"

"Too bloody busy trying not to die to make a list of things to do before I do keel over." Graham flipped absently through the pages of the book in his lap. "Not sit by the fire and wait to breathe my last, that's for fucking sure. Shag, a lot, if my cock starts working again. Travel. Do something, anything."

And how the bloody hell do I help him with that?

BC waggled his eyebrows exaggeratedly. "Well, the shagging, I can definitely help with."

CHAPTER TWENTY-ONE

GRAHAM

Aside from BC, everyone in Graham's life seemed bound and determined to do nothing but smile cheerily in his presence. He'd somehow found an incredible reserve of restraint within himself; it kept him from flinging cowpats in their faces.

They mean well, or so Freddie keeps telling me. So why do I want to shove them all over the bluff like a bunch of lemmings?

His surgery was scheduled for the end of the week. The hopes were the much simpler operation would remove all the cancer, and keep him from having a larger portion of his stomach removed. They hoped.

And prayed.

Graham had never believed much in either. His approach to life had always been impulsive, yet pragmatic.

He had never been faced with something so out of his control.

The last three days had been spent pretending nothing had changed in his life. Today, he could no longer avoid it. No matter the success or failure, he had been forever altered by everything already.

The surgery would take part of his stomach lining; better than his life, but still not completely ideal. Graham would have a few days in the hospital, plus several more on a liquid diet followed by months of chemotherapy. It might be enough.

Might.

If it weren't, he would be back in the hospital. They'd remove a portion of his stomach, which would require weeks and weeks of recovery. He didn't want to imagine it.

With his MacBook in his lap, Graham had spent the morning writing up his will. Freddie had suggested it to him. The young nurse's patients apparently felt some relief with taking care of things, having the illusion of control over at least one part of their lives.

Truth be told, there wasn't much to worry about leaving behind. He had never been one to collect things. Being constantly on the go meant not being weighed down by things. Photos, a few books, and his flat—he had nothing earth-shattering to bequeath to his loved ones.

He did write out letters. Ones that would only be read on the occasion of his death. He had penned one to BC, along with his parents, Rupert, Becca, and Francis, those most likely to be affected by his passing if the worst happened.

It might. Cancer could come back even with the surgery.

He had time now, but who knew how much of it would be granted to him.

His fingers traced the square edges of the letters on the keyboard. Graham finished tapping out the last line of the final letter. He saved it and pulled up the one to BC, checking over it for mistakes.

BC.

They'd come a long way since their first meeting in the closet during the wedding. Graham had believed it would never evolve beyond more than a fling, even a prolonged one. He couldn't imagine settling down, nor could BC, not at the time.

And yet, BC hadn't left his side even once through this nightmare. He read to him in the evenings. One room in his inn had been permanently altered just for Graham's use.

Those dark blue eyes would follow him whenever he chose to go for a short walk. BC obviously worried, but never smothered him with it. It was a relief, since his family tended to practically bury him in their concern.

"Ready for tea?" BC poked his head into the room, drawing Graham out of his thoughts. "Mrs Morgan made those ginger cakes you like so much."

"I like them because they don't make me ill." He closed his computer and set it on the bed. "Help me up? Legs aren't cooperating for shit today."

His knees tended to give out on him at the worst times. Graham had found himself pitching straight into the loo a few days ago. BC had given himself a sore throat laughing—after saving him from drowning, of course.

It had been the last time his muscled caretaker had allowed him to bathe alone. Graham drew the line at having an audience while taking a piss. He did keep one hand on a wall for support at all times; he couldn't afford a hospital stay for a concussion on top of cancer.

Graham wrapped his arm around BC's waist when the man lifted him up off the mattress on his feet. "Tea inside, or outside?"

"Outside. Fresh air is good for you."

The last few days had been so wet they hadn't ventured beyond the inn much. Bad weather made it impossible. Any bit of rain made Graham as cold as if his feet had been shoved in a glacier.

Half a piece of ginger cake later, Graham's appetite failed him. Most days it seemed he could barely manage enough to take his medication. Nausea would compound upon itself, so he nibbled bits of food and sipped tea so weak it could've been nothing more than milky water.

"I look like a sodding plonker." Graham brushed the crumbs from his gloves. "Who wears a sodding knit hat and gloves in the middle of summer to have tea in the garden?"

"Are you cold?" BC waited for him to nod his answer before continuing. "Don't worry about the twits who have so much time on their hands that they can afford to give a shit about a bloke wearing gloves in May."

Graham dropped his forehead on his arms to rest it on the table. "Can't I pretend everything is fine?"

"Sure, until we have to go to the hospital for your surgery." BC's hand landed on his head and began to gently massage his scalp. "You'll be fine. I'll be here for you, even if you aren't."

"Spoilsport." He lifted one arm to give him a one-fingered salute. "Bastard."

CHAPTER TWENTY-TWO

BC

I can do this. I can do this. I can be comforting and strong. Graham needs me to get him through his surgery. I will do it without breaking apart like the waves on the rocks on the beach.

I. Can. Do. This.

BC stared tiredly at his reflection in the bathroom mirror. He'd gotten up two hours early to prepare for the trip to Plymouth. *Nervous? Never.* Caddock had offered to play chauffeur, but Graham had finally stood his ground to say no; he didn't want a circus of an audience for his surgery.

The hardest to convince had been Rupert and Becca. They'd both tried to insist on at least meeting up in Plymouth. An exhausting argument had ensued before they caved to the wishes of the man going for surgery.

They cared. BC had tried not to shove his oar into the mix, leaving it to Graham to fight his own battles. He had dragged Rupert to the side afterwards to tell him off.

The best thing everyone could do for the ill man was to respect his wishes. If he didn't want the entire village at the hospital, they'd have to deal with it. He had enough going on without worrying about the hurt feelings of those around him.

Rupert had been stubborn. Not that BC blamed him, not really. His twin brother had been faced with his mortality. It had shaken everyone up.

"I'm dressed." Graham sat in one of the spare chairs in the kitchen, clutching a cup of tea desperately. "Aren't you impressed?"

"At your ability to clothe yourself or rhyme?" He reached over to snatch one of the scones on the table. "Ready to go?"

"Not even close."

The name of the game appeared to be procrastination, given how Graham managed to do everything possible to delay their leaving the inn. BC eventually had to resort to carrying him out to the vehicle; he'd already packed the one bag they were taking with them for the night at the hospital.

Of the treatment options, the endoscopic resection sounded the least intrusive and frightening to both of them. BC tried to console Graham with all the information Freddie had left with them. He did nothing but gaze blankly out at the passing scenery, not even acknowledging words had been spoken in his general vicinity.

All too soon, they arrived in Plymouth. The doctor went

over all the last-minute details before leaving them to settle in one of the private recovery rooms. It would be home for the next day or two, depending on how well the surgery went.

He sat beside the hospital bed with Graham's hand in his and glanced over to catch the man's eye. "So, did you see this coming when we wanked in the closet at the wedding?"

Graham burst out laughing, drawing the attention of the nearby nurses. "You complete and utter wanker."

"A bit redundant, isn't it? The wanking wanker?" BC ran his thumb over the dry, trembling fingers. He'd have to lotion Graham's skin again. It had started cracking, thanks to his treatments. "Mouths were involved."

"I don't remember mouths being involved, though consider me suitably distracted." Graham's laughter had added a healthy flush to his previously starkly pale face. His fingers shook less noticeably as well. He clutched at BC's hand. "I didn't see any of this happening—not you, not sodding cancer, either."

"Hoping I'm not in the same category." BC grunted when Graham swung a pillow around to catch him in the face. "I can't tell if that's a yes or a no. Care to elaborate?"

Any retort on Graham's lips vanished when the doctor returned. The time had apparently come. The nurses prepared their patient before whisking him away on a gurney for surgery.

BC found his hand hovering in the air where he'd been holding on to Graham only moments earlier. *Shit.* His arm dropped to his side. He couldn't pull his eyes away from the now empty bed.

Silence reigned briefly. The hushed yet chaotic sounds of a busy hospital ward barely registered. All of his attention was centred on the bed and the suddenly quiet monitoring equipment.

Well, Judas Priest, what the hell am I supposed to do now?

Ten minutes went by so slowly he had to check his watch, phone, and the clock on the wall to confirm it had only been that long. He flipped through all the channels on the telly. *Nothing, another five minutes wasted.* This would definitely be the longest day of his life thus far.

He went for a walk outside the hospital. His path took him around the buildings and parking garage twice. He returned to the room after a while with a fresh cup of tea.

No news.

Is no news good or bad?

Several excruciating hours went by in what felt more like four days. The nurses eventually brought their groggy patient back into the room. They moved him efficiently to the bed and left without a word once he'd been hooked up to the monitors.

Freddie popped in to check up on them both. "He'll be coming out of his anaesthesia soon. He's likely to be a bit out of it for a while. Try not to laugh too hard at him."

"Laugh? Not sure I can remember how." BC frowned in disbelief at the young nurse. He didn't have to wait too long to discover what exactly Freddie had meant.

"Wankity wanker wanks wankily." Graham's whisper drew him out of the book he'd been reading.

BC could only stare at him in bewildered amusement. *Freddie should've been more specific.* He did have the rather inappropriate urge to laugh. "Does he? What does he wank?"

"Wanker," he shouted triumphantly. His green eyes were glazed over and unfocused. "Wanks. Wanker. Wank?"

"Maybe not so loud? I don't think the children's ward needs to hear you." BC glanced towards the door, half expecting the uptight head nurse to rush in and whack them with a ruler for being naughty. "Why don't you take a nap?"

"Sod naps."

"Right." BC grabbed his phone to film the babbling redhead. He might as well record it for posterity. Graham would find it hilarious to watch later. "So, tell me all about this wanking business."

Ten minutes of blackmail-worthy video later, Graham had dozed off on the bed. BC shut his phone down. He could share the wealth later; Rupert would likely bust his spleen laughing.

While his wanderer rested, BC snuck out to find Genevieve. She updated him on how it had gone. They believed all of the cancer had been gotten out of his stomach lining, but they'd be monitoring it to make sure.

And more chemotherapy—of course.

Genevieve cautioned him not to worry when it got worse before it got better. *Not reassuring, Doctor, not even a little bit.* She also mentioned additional testing that would come late in July or early August. They had to ensure the damaged tissue had all been removed. Graham would be back in to have additional surgery if it wasn't.

Not a terrifying thought at all. Why am I here? I'm not sodding family. Am I? Do I want to be?

I do.

Shit.

After an uncomfortable night in Plymouth, they returned to the Fisherman's Refuge. Family and a liquid diet awaited them—or Graham, at least. BC remained outside, allowing the others a chance to grill Ginger Spice on the details of how things had gone.

He sat on the front steps, not even noticing the rain drizzling on his shoes. "You're in over your damned head, you numpty."

"Admitting it is the first step to recovery." Becca squeezed into the space between him and the railing. "You've been a solid rock for our traveller. We haven't bothered to check in on how you're dealing with everything."

"I'm fine."

"Says the bloke sitting outside in the rain?" She tilted her head to the side with both eyebrows raised dubiously. "Go on, pull the other one."

"No thanks." BC scratched absently at the hair on his cheek; he was overdue a bit of a shave. "I'm trying to figure out how this turned into a relationship when both of us are shit at them. We do sex, not feelings. When did it change? Did it? I'm sodding hallucinating, aren't I?"

"Nah, only if I am, and I'm fairly confident I'm not delusional." Becca's worried frown blossomed into a sly smile. She crossed her arms, shivering a bit in the rain. "Love is like the perfect summer day in London. It's never guaranteed, always worth the wait, and occasionally happens when you've given up on the clouds parting. Enjoy it. Don't run away."

Love?

Love.

Oh, Judas Priest, love.

I've gone and fallen in love.

CHAPTER TWENTY-THREE

GRAHAM

Liquid diets had to be a torture device created by the twisted mind of a sadomasochist. He had one more day. One. Odds weren't good on him surviving through it.

He had never imagined going days without having to use his teeth. He ran his tongue over them to make sure they were still there. *Yep. Good.* He winced when the move pulled on his cracking lips, another casualty of chemotherapy.

Please, God, please, real sodding food.

Solid food that wouldn't taste vile or look regurgitated. Mrs Morgan had already promised to make him something light, but tasty. He had started to count the minutes until freedom would be his, dietary-wise.

It had gotten to the point that his dreams had been filled with pasties, buns, and spotted dick. He'd never had a wet dream about food, even with the puns. A clear sign his stomach had reached the stage of revolt, particularly given that his equipment refused to work.

The other troubling issue on his mind had been the itch to travel. Graham told himself to let it go, perspective and all that. Logically he knew he wouldn't have the energy to go for months, maybe even a year.

In the grand scheme of the situation in his life, not travelling shouldn't have even been on his top ten worst things to happen. Wandering around required energy, and he barely managed to shuffle from the bed to the en-suite without help. BC had been offering his kind assistance with sponge baths.

Don't mind those now, do we?

BC, it seemed, had nothing but time for him. They'd grown increasingly reliant on and comfortable with each other. How could they not? Illness brought people closer, revealing the best and worst in them.

One of the other casualties to his illness related to BC. The man who normally kept both his head and beard neatly shaven seemed to have forgotten how to use a razor. His clothes were often rumpled—more focused on caring for Graham than himself.

The former rugby player had no limits when it came to helping with all aspects of dealing with the side effects of chemotherapy. BC wiped Graham's face after each lost battle with keeping food down. He carried him outside to enjoy rare sunny days, covered in a blanket, hat, and cardigan to stay warm.

"Sludge time." BC joined him in the library, handing

over the suspicious-looking smoothie. "Cheer up, Ginger Spice, only two more to go."

Graham stared dismally at the cup now sitting in his hand. "Shit."

BC threw himself into the chair across from Graham, almost knocking it over in the process. "How was the visit with Freddie?"

"Hyper." He couldn't think of a better word to describe his always cheerful nurse. "Like a sodding Chihuahua."

"That's Freddie for you. What did he have to say?" BC rested his hand lightly on Graham's knee. "Anything good?"

"Genevieve did scans immediately after." Graham gripped the glass even more tightly, trying to stave off fear-induced nausea. It wouldn't help him to chug down his lunch. "They want me back in Plymouth next week."

"So soon?"

"She's worried." He decided drinking the sludge would be preferable to voicing what his nurse had told him. He finished his liquid lunch and swiped his tongue with his fingers several times in a futile attempt to get the taste out of his mouth. "I'm tired. Always. Tired."

BC took the glass from him and set it on the mantle. He lifted Graham up to his feet to give him a hand walking down the hall to the bedroom. "Need the loo first?"

"No," he barked sharply. *Too sharp, really.* "Shit. Sorry."

He hadn't meant to get angry. Freddie's news had scared him. All of this terrified him, leaving him often irrationally angry.

They both flopped bonelessly onto the bed, side by side with equal gracelessness. BC shrugged off his apology. He likely thought a bit of snappishness understandable under the circumstances; Graham didn't know if he would've been as kind if the situations had been reversed.

The two men had slept together every night. Sex had been non-existent since his chemo started. Not only was Graham too tired, but he also found he couldn't perform.

The one time they'd tried had been a lesson in humiliation and kindness. BC had gone to extraordinary lengths to soothe his embarrassment. Another reason to lean heavily on the man as opposed to his brother or his parents, he didn't, to sound clichéd, sweat the small stuff.

Not once had BC pretended having cancer didn't completely suck. Everyone else wanted to push it under the rug, or pretty up the ugliness of it. Graham had gone beyond the point where that was possible. Ignoring the truth wouldn't make it go away.

Ever since his visit to the hospital, Graham had had the growing suspicion it hadn't been an entirely successful operation. He *just* knew. Freddie had only confirmed it.

Genevieve wanted him back in Plymouth for another scan. She didn't think the initial surgery had been enough. He would likely end up losing part of his stomach as well.

Not all of it. Please, God, not all of it.

"Want to talk about it?" BC asked idly, still staring up at the ceiling. "Spider in the corner is plotting our death through slow poison injected by his tiny teeth."

"Do spiders have teeth?" Graham brushed the tears that

had gathered at the corners of his eyes, masking an aborted sob with a chuckle. "Not ready for a chat."

"Good, didn't want to listen to you natter on anyway." BC sat up suddenly and glanced over at him. "I think we're overdue a *Mr Bean* marathon. I'll nosh on delicious food. You won't be able to have any of it. How brilliant will that be?"

Before Graham could exact revenge for the comment on the food, BC bounded out of the room. He returned with extra pillows, a stack of DVDs, and one of the soft quilts from the library.

My favourite one, the soppy plonker.

From the crumbs on his shirt, BC had eaten in the kitchen. He tended to avoid shoving what Graham couldn't have into his face. He might joke about it, but he never did it.

Sleep didn't come easily to Graham after their impromptu Rowan Atkinson fest. He usually napped throughout the day and night. Chemo had made him tired, yet at the same time caused him to struggle with insomnia. Nausea didn't do anything to help him drift off; neither did all of his aches and pains.

He could hear Freddie nattering in his ear. *"Stress hurts your recovery."* What part of the entire process wasn't anxiety causing? He might as well have told him not to breathe, take a piss, or wank.

Oh, wait, I can't sodding get it up either.

Rolling to the edge of the bed, Graham went through the painful process of getting to his feet. He had strength; his knees didn't seem to know it. His fingers went from the nightstand to a shelf, and finally to the wall to keep himself upright.

He made it through the dimly lit inn on his fool's errand for tea and ginger biscuits. If dunked in the hot liquid, the soft cookie should go down smoothly. It might only be two in the morning, but technically today was to be his first day back on solids.

Solids, of a sort. Are eggs solid? Soft foods have to taste better than the shit smoothie from hell, right? Please, God, it can't be worse.

The chair by the range that Mrs Morgan often used called his name. Graham would've patted himself on the back for making it over to sit down if he'd only had the energy. He gulped in air, trying not to swoon like a ninny.

Pawing on his leg drew his attention to Zeus, who had followed him on the night-time adventure. The Yorkie continued to badger him until he was lifted up. Graham almost pitched forward out of the chair in the process.

Death by mini menace.

After remembering what balance meant and how to breathe, Graham left Zeus in the chair and started to make tea. Pure willpower kept him on his feet, going through the motions. He'd have his tea.

Or bloody well make a massive mess in the process of failing.

"Sudden craving?"

Graham started so badly he almost dropped the hot cup of tea. He barely managed to set it down safely on the counter. "If you make me spill this after all it took to fix it, I'll have you by the balls."

"Have you boiled enough water for two?" BC shuffled

over, giving Zeus a side-eyed scowl before reaching up into the cupboard for a cup for himself. "Do you often find yourself wanting tea at half past three?"

"Biscuits." He used a spoon to avoid the cookie disintegrating on him. "Mushy, but better than the healthy sludge I've been force-fed for days."

"So, tell me about Freddie, Ginger Spice."

"Young bloke, bit too handsome for his own good, hair on his chin—mostly to ensure he looks old enough to drive." Graham stopped when a tea towel gently landed across his head. He tugged it off. "Yes?"

"What did Freddie tell you?"

"Ahh." Graham shoved the cup and saucer away. He rested his arms on the table, allowing his chin to drop on top of them. "They might not have removed all the cancerous tissue."

"Shit."

"Precisely."

BC budged over to sit beside him, draping one heavy arm across Graham's shoulders. "What do we do now? More tests? Another surgery? Chemo?"

"Not sure yet. Yes? Maybe? All of the above?" Graham leant into the larger man's strength. He felt no shame in wanting, needing, the comfort. "What if I'm in the 20 percent instead of the eighty?"

BC had to clear his throat harshly to answer. He still sounded a bit off to Graham when he did speak. "A rather wise woman told me not to borrow my sorrows from tomorrow. If you are, I'll take you anywhere in the world you want to go.

We'll travel for as long as you want—or can."

"One last adventure?"

"Worst-case scenario only." BC always managed to sound so hopeful while never running away from the potentially dismal truth. "Wait for tests before you have me planning where to scatter your ashes, all right?"

"Bastard."

They sat holding each other in the kitchen until Mrs Morgan came bustling in at six in the morning. She didn't even blink at the sight of them. They had fresh tea and breakfast faster than Graham could've managed.

He attempted his first real meal in ages and made a promise to himself. This wouldn't conquer him no matter what. It couldn't, not with friends, family, and BC beside him.

Freddie had warned him not to panic. They didn't have a complete answer for what might have happened. None of the doctors could say for certain yet how much cancer remained.

What if I die? Fuck. What if I'm dying—no, don't panic. Even if it's not the worst, I'm going to make every sodding minute count, whether I die in a year or in twenty.

CHAPTER TWENTY-FOUR

BC

By mid-July, BC had driven back and forth to Plymouth multiple times. He knew the route well enough to do it blindfolded. One test had followed another, each requiring a two-hour trip to get there and back.

The eventual conclusion from Graham's team of specialists came the third week in the month. Genevieve had delivered the news as gently as possible. Surgery to remove a portion of his stomach would happen in August.

Bad news combined with a stronger dose of chemo to make Graham both listless and depressed, and no one could blame him. A steady stream of visitors attempting to cheer him up hadn't helped. Rupert's last visit had ended in angry tears from both twins; the older ginger hadn't been back since the fight.

Freddie had been by several times, including early in the morning. He'd brought with him a new diet plan, updated medications, and a schedule for the upcoming surgery complete with hospital stay and projected recovery time. As a result, Graham had gone straight to bed afterwards with Zeus curled up on a pillow beside him.

The dog had proven to be the one thing almost guaranteed to lighten the sick man's mood. It made BC appreciate the dog, although he could've done without him in their bed and waking up with a mouthful of fur each morning.

"I've put a haddock chowder on the hob for lunch with cheddar toasties. Will your young man want some?" Mrs Morgan stepped up beside him and placed a cup of hot coffee in his hand. "Drink up, poppet. We'll get you through this."

"One can only hope." He lifted the mug up to salute her. "Ta, for the coffee. I'll see if I can't get the ginger grump out of his bed."

"You leave him to me, poppet."

Ten minutes later, a pyjama-clad Graham sat at the kitchen table glaring tiredly at anyone who dared speak to him. He ate, not much, but enough. His attempt to escape immediately after failed when BC quickly blocked his path.

"You need some fresh air."

"I don't *need* sodding fresh air." Graham sounded stronger than he was. He couldn't shove off BC, who lifted him up easily to carry him outside. "Oi! Put me down, you boorish bastard. What are you doing?"

The Cornish sun shone brightly enough for the two of them to blink rapidly to clear their vision. They made their way out to the stone bench set up at the top of the bluff. Blankets had already been set out earlier; the things ended up all over the inn.

BC wrapped a few of the quilts around his captive to keep him warm. "Beautiful day, isn't it?"

Nothing.

Amidst the mild wind, they could catch the sound of the children playing on the beach far below them. The two men sat in relatively companionable silence. *Fairly friendly.* Graham huffed a few times angrily before settling himself down.

"Why are you doing all of this?" Graham voiced the question he'd expressed several times already over the passing months. "No one plays nurse for a quick shag. You don't have some caretaker fetish, do you? Pervy bastard that you are."

Now's the time. Say it. Tell him how you feel. Life's short, isn't it? So spit it out, Brooks. He might be a dying man, so he can only laugh at you for a limited time.

"Always wanted to play doctor." BC mentally cursed his cowardice and focused on a cloud oddly shaped almost exactly like a rugby ball while preparing to bare his soul. "I love you."

Graham appeared to freeze in place. His teeth worried at his bottom lip before he finally responded. "No, you don't."

"Yes, I sodding do." He hadn't come this far to be summarily dismissed without being heard or believed. "I understand that the pain, humiliation, and upheaval are part of the package."

"Sounds like something Francis would say." Graham gave him a pained grimace. "Well, bugger it all, I love you too."

"Shit." BC rubbed a hand over the stubble covering his head. He should've borrowed one of the many hats Graham had started collecting since losing his hair. "We could've planned our timing better. Who architects falling in love?"

"People who aren't idiotic numpties or individuals who aren't facing death." Graham gave a slow shake of his head. "We're going to be awful at this love thing, aren't we?"

"Total shit at it." BC forced a smile through the tears that had gathered in his eyes.

CHAPTER TWENTY-FIVE

GRAHAM

The dark clouds over Graham had slowly dispersed with the days slowly marching towards August. The shock from the news of yet another surgery eventually faded into a sense of numb acceptance. Why fight against the inevitable?

Part of his stomach would be taken. He couldn't magically alter the situation with a snap of his fingers. It was a case of facing the facts head-on without too much flinching.

His brother had always told him the key to a successful rugby try in a difficult match was to never flinch in the face of a larger foe. He couldn't readily imagine a greater opponent to conquer than cancer. He'd do it.

Or I'll die trying.

He had to laugh. Illness had certainly brought out the darker elements of his humour. It was the fatalistic side that his brother couldn't understand.

Rupert had practically screamed at him over it. "Why aren't you taking this seriously?" Graham didn't believe anyone could honestly accuse him of not taking his mortality gravely. Pun intended. Moping about the situation hadn't gotten him anywhere. Should he shout at his doctors, rail at God, and grump at everyone within hearing distance?

What would any of it accomplish? He'd still have cancer and be heading for surgery. His chances of dying would've gone up massively with or without a show of temper.

The emotional upheaval tired him more in some ways than the treatments did. He'd eventually decided to simply let it go. Maintaining high levels of angst wasn't his style.

Each day, Graham made the journey up the bluff to sit on the bench. *His bench.* Sometimes help was required to make it up there. He wouldn't give up until his body flatlined, maybe not even then.

Definitely not even then.

He had to fight. Freddie brought him to a therapy group once a week to meet others who were in various stages of having cancer. They all agreed on the importance of not giving up.

Never.

You give up, you die.

I don't want to die.

The wet nose of a Shetland sheepdog was the first clue someone had joined him on top of the hill. Francis sat next to him with Sherlock circling around them. The dog finally made himself comfortable at their feet.

"Are you well? Rupert's been nothing but gloom and doom since you fought." Francis loosened his bow tie in the summer heat, folding it carefully to place in his front pocket. "He didn't mean what he said. Your brother's afraid of losing you. It's all any of us have thought about for months."

"I know, Francis." Graham didn't have the energy for his own fight *and* dealing with everyone else's fears. "I'm aware it's hard for all of you. It's not fair of me, but he has to be the one to reach out. I can't. I've got to sodding live. All my reserves are going towards it. I've *got* to beat this thing. I've found someone, Francis. He's a stupid plonker most of the time, but he's brilliant. And. I. Can't. Die. So I'd be ever so grateful if you'd tell my bloody brother to bugger off. How can he not see why I might need a good laugh right about now without feeling guilty? I'm taking my decreasing chances of survival as seriously as I can. What does he want me to do?"

Sherlock chose to demonstrate his therapy dog training. He sat up and placed his head on Graham's knee. The sheepdog appeared completely content to stay there and be petted.

"BC is a good man." Francis smiled affectionately at his dog. "Sherlock likes him. He's always been a rather excellent judge of character. He hated all the men I dated before Caddock."

"Everyone hated the blokes before your husband." Graham smirked at him when he huffed indignantly. "Or so your gran tells me."

"She lies and gossips."

"Right." Graham chuckled. He ran his fingers through the dog's fur. "Tell my twin to stop being a stubborn twit. If he wants to see me so badly, he can jolly well drag his arse up here."

Francis leant his head against Graham's shoulder. "We'll let Rupert stew in his thoughts for a few days."

"Long enough for Joanne to lose patience with him?"

"Exactly."

They enjoyed the calm morning air. Sherlock eventually returned to his previous spot, stretched out across their feet. His ears stayed perked up as though listening for any signs of distress from either man.

"Have you told BC about all these feelings you've bottled up?" His best mate from childhood and university appeared far too amused for his liking. "I know you've been naughty with each other—and at my wedding as well. You dirty, dirty boys."

Shit.

"Who told on us?" Graham flushed bright red and had to turn away from the laughing man at his side. "Wait. Don't tell me, Rupert."

"He didn't." Francis's eyes twinkled with easy merriment. "I spotted you two ducking into a closet together. How utterly thrilling it was."

"You were thrilled?" Graham snorted in amusement. "We've buggered all over the inn at this point."

Francis glanced him over from head to toe. "I'm quite certain Mrs Morgan regularly sanitises all flat surfaces, but I'll make sure not to eat off the table without a plate. Maybe I should bring a handkerchief to sit on?"

It only took one look at each other to fall into silly giggles. Graham found himself reminded of the time they'd been in class at university and their professor's trousers had ripped to reveal heart-covered pants. He reached over to take his old friend's slender hand in his own.

He'd missed him. Francis had an infectious lightness to his personality. He drew others in with it, probably what had attracted Caddock to him.

"I don't want to die yet." Graham swallowed hard to stem the sudden tears threatening to fall. "Not when I've found a man who can laugh through life with me. We said I love you, but I'm not sure he knows how deeply I meant it."

Francis placed his other hand over their joined ones. "It's a terrifying thing, being in love."

"Dying's not brilliant either."

"No, but you're not ashes yet, Graham Hodson. You hear me?" Francis squeezed his fingers to the point of almost causing pain. "You shouldn't pen a farewell letter until you know the journey is guaranteed."

"Stay in the present?"

"It can't hurt."

"No, I suppose it can't." Graham had to chuckle when Sherlock sat up to rest his chin on their hands. "I think your nutty canine agrees with you. How do you put up with him?"

"He's brilliant, he is." Francis always gushed about his dog like a proud father. "You leave my Sherlock alone. He's perfect."

Graham found himself remembering Caddock's little nephew who lived with them. He hadn't seen the boy since the wedding. "How's little Devlin doing? Has he settled in with you two?"

"Better. His speech is where it should be for being almost five. He's in therapy once a week to help with losing his father." Francis tilted his head to rest against his friend's shoulder. "Being a father, even if it's more guardian than anything, is an odd business."

"How so?"

"You learn quickly to pick your battles and what's important." He remained silent for almost a minute, and Graham waited patiently for him to continue. "Life's short, with or without cancer added to the mix. If you've only got months or years, enjoy it with BC. Leave him with all the precious memories you can. You'll only have regrets if you don't."

"Did you come here with the sole purpose of making me sob like an infant?" Graham scrubbed impatiently at his eyes.

"What are best mates for?"

CHAPTER TWENTY-SIX

BC

"If the two of you flutter your lashes at each other over my treacle tart one more time, I think the room might spontaneously combust." Mrs Morgan waved her fork at the two men sharing lunch with her. She pointed the utensil at Graham. "He'll be in surgery in two days, so why don't you spill the beans now, all right? I'd rather not die from the suspense of it all, poppets."

Flutter eyelashes?

BC exchanged an amused grin with Graham. "Yes, Mrs Morgan."

Graham threw a piece of crust at the man as he widened his eyes and pretended to swoon. "*Arse.*"

"No cursing at my table."

"Yes, Mrs Morgan." Graham gave a weak kick to BC's shin under the table.

The second she'd left to see to the few guests at the inn, BC burst into peals of laughter. Graham followed him into it readily. The amusement acted like the release of a pressure cooker, steaming away the strain of worry from the last few weeks.

July had gone by far too quickly. The date of surgery had all but snuck up on them. They felt completely prepared and lost in loose ends at the same time.

They'd driven to Plymouth to meet with both Freddie and Genevieve to discuss all the minute details of the operation. It had been hard to listen to the odds of it going catastrophically wrong. All of it made BC want to cover his ears to block out their words.

He couldn't. Reality wouldn't go away because he refused to listen. It hadn't in the past when he'd tried ignoring all the signs of his career going down the loo.

He couldn't give up.

Graham certainly hadn't. Ill, pale, and increasingly frail, he had shown immense courage through all of it. One unpleasant aspect of cancer after another, but nothing brought him permanently to his knees.

Even living on bits of food and popsicles, Graham managed to keep his spirits up, at least a little. He flagged every once in a while. Those were the times when BC swept in to try to make him laugh, or hold his hand.

"You okay, book sniffer?"

BC shook his head to clear his thoughts. "I'm fine."

Graham pushed his half-eaten meal across the table. "I haven't had my walk today. Go with me? Freddie won't be coming again this week, not with my appointment at the hospital coming up soon."

"You just want a BC-sized walking stick." He offered his arm for support to help him up to his feet. "Off we go into the waiting Cornish air."

The summer had been unseasonably mild, one of the mildest on record. Mrs Morgan had claimed it an answer to her prayers for some small comfort for the ailing Graham. BC didn't know if he believed in divine intervention, but the sun and ocean air had done the redhead good.

"I've never loved a place enough to want to call it home permanently." Graham sank down on the bench. He sounded exhausted from the short jaunt from the inn up to the top of the bluff. "It's wonderful here. Sonnets could be written about the salty sea air."

"My family knew what they were about." BC had slowly begun to appreciate the beauty of the bay, the inn, and the people. "A wonderful life could be lived up here."

"Yes." Graham rubbed his hands together before tucking them into his ever-present quilt. "If I can't beat this thing, I would love—"

"Don't." He waved his hand sharply to cut him off midsentence. "There's no cause to risk inciting fate. *Judas Priest.* Freddie said to stay positive."

"Positive, yes. He didn't mention turning into an oblivious-to-the-truth twit." Graham adjusted his hat when the wind shifted it slightly. "You've been my pillar of truth up to this point. Don't start shitting false platitudes all over me now."

BC closed his eyes against the images of Graham's death, which had haunted him for days. He forced a steadiness into his voice, one he didn't feel. "Just make sure you leave your laptop to me. It's the only thing you own worth any money."

All too soon for both men, the day of surgery was upon them. Graham hadn't slept a wink, nor had BC, who sat up with him throughout the night. They'd wanted to draw out their time together.

Just in case.

They'd settled in the library, reading from yet another book that had been on their to-be-read lists. They'd drunk enough tea to drown half the country. Yet, still, neither of them felt prepared for the coming operation.

Several hours later, BC stood side by side with Graham, staring up at the hospital. Neither of them could find words. They stayed holding hands for almost ten minutes.

"Surgery can't happen out here, lads." Freddie walked up behind them. "In we go now, the team is already prepped and waiting for you."

"Over the top with us?" BC wrapped an arm around Graham's shoulders and wasn't surprised to find them trembling. "Why don't we have a quick snog in an empty room? Better to die happy than not."

"*Arse.*"

As BC wasn't family or a spouse, he'd been relegated to the high dependency unit where Graham would end up post-surgery. Genevieve, as head doctor, kept him informed. Hospital policy, however, kept him from being closer to where the now sedated patient had been whisked off.

The hustle and bustle of the high dependency unit surprised BC. He'd thought, after a major operation, a patient would want calm and quiet. The area hummed with an immense level of activity, nurses rushing around to see to their charges.

BC paced. He sat. He flicked through an endless supply of magazines without reading a word or even seeing the pictures inside of them.

As time went by, Graham's friends and family began to show up; the small waiting room filled up quickly. The sick man would have been chuffed at the attention if he'd been conscious. He'd also likely have attempted to toss everyone out on their ear—his Ginger Spice was a complex individual.

"He'll be fine." Caddock dropped into the seat beside him, making it creak worryingly. BC smirked at him, and he glared in return. "One crack about my weight and I'm dragging you outside to kick your arse."

"As if you could. The Brute never once managed to get the better of me on the pitch." BC crossed his arms and chuckled at the now grumbling man. "That's what I thought. Are you here for a reason? Or merely to goad me into forgetting the fact that the man I've suddenly found myself in love with is in the middle of surgery to save his life?"

Caddock raised his eyebrows in a perfect picture of surprise. "I had no bloody idea you knew words larger than shit and arse."

"Francis." BC leaned forward to see around the oversized idiot seated beside him. "Could you collect your husband before I collect his head?"

"Why don't you and Rupert round up some coffees for everyone?" Francis stared pointedly at his husband and plopped into the chair he vacated. "He means well."

BC gave a wry chuckle. "I'm well aware. Caddock has about as much grace and tact as I do, which means he's total shit at it."

"If I ask how you're doing, will you bite my head off?"

BC had to laugh at the absurdity of the idea of hurting the slender dandy. "No, I wouldn't, and not only because your husband and my ginger would both have my balls on a platter if I dared to raise my voice at you."

"You'd have to get by Sherlock in any case."

"Where is the mutt wonder?" BC couldn't recall ever seeing the interior designer without his constant canine companion. "He's a service dog, right? They'd let him into the hospital."

"Gran's watching him." Francis straightened his bow tie. He sniffed at the empty cup in his hand. "More tea?"

"Not for me."

With Rupert and the Hodsons there, BC had been shunted off to the side in favour of immediate family by many of the staff. He wanted to complain about it, but it seemed wrong to make a scene. Waiting for an answer hadn't ever killed anyone, after all.

He doubted Rupert would keep any news on his twin from him; the man had appreciated BC being there for his brother while Rupert had struggled to process everything. He hoped. They all seemed to understand the depths his relationship with Graham had grown to over the last few months.

Feeling far too much like a caged animal, BC decided to walk the hospital halls. No one stopped him during his first circuit of the corridors. He headed down a floor to find a cup of tea; too much coffee already had his nerves even more on edge than the operation.

"BC!"

He paused with the paper cup halfway to his lips at Caddock's shout. He turned towards the man with a disapproving scowl. "Nurses will probably frown on you shouting like a hooligan."

Caddock shrugged off the scolding. "Graham's out of surgery. Doctor grabbed the Hodson clan to fill them in on how it went."

The whoosh from the nearby sliding door was about all BC heard after Caddock's first words. Graham had survived his operation, the first of the many hurdles facing them in the fight against cancer. He jogged by his former teammate and down the hall to find either Freddie or Genevieve, who would be more likely to share with him.

"BC?" Freddie caught him by the arm when he started to stride past the nurses' station. "The doctors are all in a conference with the family."

"Can you tell me anything?" BC pulled in his temper by the skin of his teeth. It wasn't the young man's fault the system didn't consider him a part of Graham's family, even if he'd been the one to care for the man since his diagnosis. "*Shit.* I'm sure Rupert will happily tell me how his brother is doing, but I'm not sure my patience will handle the wait."

"He'll be in recovery for several hours, waking up and allowing them to assess where his level of pain and awareness is. It's likely he'll be sitting up by the end of the day. If everything continues to go smoothly, he'll be in his private room tomorrow morning at the latest." Freddie placed a hand on BC's arm in an obvious attempt to offer comfort. "It went well—as well as it could've gone."

"He'll be fine?"

Freddie patted his arm gently. "It's cancer, BC. He's a long way from fine, but the doctors believe they got all of it this time."

"We have hope?" BC breathed a massive sigh of relief when the other man nodded. "Thank God."

CHAPTER TWENTY-SEVEN

GRAHAM

Brightness and subdued voices brought him to a state of alertness. Graham panicked initially when opening his eyelids felt almost like swimming through treacle. It took a number of tries to open his eyes fully, and even then the sudden intense light only made him want to close them.

The various tubes in him didn't help his sudden urge to freak out. One of the nurses murmured comfortingly to him, reminding him where he was—and why he was there. It helped, a little at least, given his unfocused mind.

As the haze from anaesthesia faded, the fog from pain medication picked up. His mother drifted in along with his father; Graham couldn't understand half of what they said. He did feel her frail hand trembling when she clutched gently at his fingers.

Rupert came next, and his twin had the audacity to take a selfie with him completely out of it in the hospital bed. Graham would have to remember to return the favour in kind. His mother rushed in to scold his slightly older brother, boxing him about the ears with her purse.

His eyes closed though he tried to fight it, wanting to see one particular person. He drifted in and out through the day, barely cognizant of Genevieve checking on him. Pain medication always did a number on him.

The next time he awoke to find himself in a private room. BC sat beside his bed, slumped down in a chair, snoring loudly. Graham glanced towards the clock on the wall to see he'd been out for almost a day.

A book resting on top of the blanket caught his attention, *H is for Hawk*, a story by Helen Macdonald that had been recommended by Eric Idle on his website. The two men had started to work their way through some of the novels on the Monty Python star's massive list. Graham had been the one to suggest this one next.

A shame I was too sodding drugged out to remember whatever he read to me.

Taking advantage of the brief moment of solitude, Graham attempted to sit up slowly. The wires and tubing still attached to him made it nigh on impossible. He huffed in sheer annoyance at them.

Freddie had gone into great detail with him a week prior to surgery on what he should expect. Even knowing all of it, Graham struggled not to yank on the tubes. He wanted them all gone.

For several days, Graham suffered the indignity of being fed via a tube. He also had a catheter, which Rupert had taken the mickey about several times. It had almost been worth the humiliation to watch his mother once again bash his twin about with her purse.

Almost.

Over the course of the next week, Genevieve slowly allowed him to return to normalcy. Graham had never felt more grateful than when all the wiring attached to his body had finally been removed. He had a far greater appreciation for all the poor souls living with tubes to feed them than ever before.

His doctor, along with Freddie, had reiterated the strict diet he would need to follow for months, along with the additional rounds of chemotherapy. They wanted to make certain the cancer was gone. Genevieve had sounded more confident than after his previous operation when she stated they believed all of it had been removed.

By the middle of the second week of recovery, Graham had been allowed to leave the hospital. Caddock had driven up in his oversized Range Rover—far more comfortable for him than anyone else's vehicle would be. The former rugby player, now pub owner, had waved off his thanks.

BC had barely left his side in the hospital. Even now he sat next to Graham in the vehicle with a bag full of medicine, vitamins, and instructions from Freddie. The young nurse coordinator would be out to visit later in the week.

"Welcome home, poppet. Let's get you inside. You look rather done in." Mrs Morgan escorted them into the inn and helped get him safely and comfortably ensconced in bed with pillows behind him for support. "Now you give me all those papers on the diet plan so I can make sure we've got everything you'll need."

"I don't want to be a bother." Graham had taken an extra-strong dose of his pain medication at the hospital in preparation for the journey to Torpoint. It made him drowsy, and he found himself struggling not to doze off midsentence. "BC? Give me a hand down will you?"

Moving quickly over to the bed, BC helped ease him down on the mattress. Graham would have to thank him later, somehow, for everything he'd done for him. He fell asleep with the former rugby player's fingers gently caressing his bald head.

Sleeping through most of the day and night did wonders for his mood; Graham woke the next morning hungry for the first time in ages. He would be on small, frequent meals for the next few months. Freddie had worked carefully to ensure the foods not only encouraged him to eat, but also helped him regain some of the weight and strength lost.

"You up, Ginger Spice? I thought I'd wake you up with breakfast." BC stepped into the room, setting a tray on the foot of the bed and rushing over to help him sit up. "You doing all right?"

"Not a clue, not a sodding Scooby-Doo." Graham longed to be able to reach up to scratch the back of his neck, but the scars from his surgery were still a tad too sore to stretch too much. "Better? Maybe? Shit. I'm hungry, that's good-ish news."

BC brightened immediately. "Mrs Morgan made scrambled eggs with soft cheese plus a peanut butter and banana smoothie with yoghurt in it. Remember, Freddie said small bites, no gorging yourself."

"Couldn't if I wanted to." Graham's appetite hadn't been stable since he'd begun chemotherapy. He did find it encouraging how the smell of eggs made him even hungrier. "Hand it over then."

BC snickered at him before handing over the glass and shifting the tray further up the bed. "Try not to vomit on it—or me. I'll give you a sponge bath later if you're a good lad."

"Book-sniffing arse."

"Sounds far kinkier than it is."

"Always does."

CHAPTER TWENTY-EIGHT

BC

"I haven't wanked in months," BC commented idly in the middle of lunch, causing Graham to spit mashed potato all over himself. He laughed at the scowling ginger and tossed him a napkin. "You're in a right state."

"*Plonker.*" Graham flicked a clump of potato at him. "You could've waited until I'd finished chewing."

"It's a bit generous to call it chewing when most of your food's soft and squishy." BC had to chuckle at the grimace sent his way. "You've been on solids for days now, cheer up."

They'd been back from Plymouth for a few weeks. Graham had settled into his new diet. His recovery had been going brilliantly, so well they all worried about the other shoe dropping.

The sponge baths were by far the best and worst part

of his day. Graham's naked body, even ill and frail, did wonderful things to BC. He struggled not to let his hands stray unnecessarily, not wanting to excite either of them when nothing would come of it.

"You're thinking about the sponge baths." Graham grinned.

BC ignored the knowing smirk aimed in his direction. "My favourite part of the day."

As the dose of his chemo lessened, Graham had slowly begun to feel healthy again. He still had months and months to go to consider himself fully recovered, but the improvements thus far had lifted both of their spirits.

His last treatment would be sometime in November if all continued to go well. Graham had spoken quite a bit about how he hoped his hair would grow back quickly. The unspoken desire of both of them related directly to his libido returning; neither of them had enjoyed sexual pleasure for far too long.

It wasn't that BC hadn't been capable of it. On the contrary, his cock had been hard enough to drill through the wall just the night before last, but it didn't seem right to indulge when Graham couldn't. He'd turned into a right soppy numpty.

"I'm all full up." Graham shoved his plate away in disgust. "Will I ever eat like a normal person again?"

"Not completely, not for a long while."

"Lie to me."

BC couldn't resist the sudden painful vulnerability in those typically vibrant green eyes. "You'll soon be noshing on any number of weird concoctions from around the world, more than you could ever dream of, in no time at all. *Judas Priest.* Give yourself time to get there. You lost part of your stomach. It's slightly more significant than having a tooth yanked. Don't lose hope now that we've finally gotten within reach of the finish line. *Idiot.*"

"Only slightly more significant?" Graham's smile was a bit watery but there nonetheless. His moods had frequently vacillated up and down since his operation. Freddie had warned all of them about it being a natural part of the process. "Keep telling myself to have patience."

"You're due a vitamin shot tomorrow." BC kept a watch on the vitamin B12 injections and other medications Graham had to take. He had a diary Freddie had made up for him to keep track of it all. "Freddie'll be out for it. Thank God. I hate giving you those bloody things."

"Is the great BC afraid of needles?"

"Shut it." BC wasn't afraid of them. It had more to do with not wanting to cause the man any additional pain. "Need a piss? It's time for your walk, and I wouldn't want you to have an accident on the way."

"Come closer, so I can give you a swift kick in the arse." Graham beckoned to him with a grin. "Well?"

"Why waste the energy? You'd only hurt yourself."

Part of getting better involved ensuring that each day Graham went a bit farther, stayed outside a bit longer. As time inched towards October and colder weather, they struggled to find times to go out when not only was it warm enough but not raining. Their jackets and brollies got plenty of use.

"Here, poppet, you'll need this." Mrs Morgan stopped them in the hallway to hand Graham an oversized jumper. "I've been knitting this for months for you."

While Graham thanked her profusely, BC helped him get it on over his shirt. He gave her his own grateful smile. Mrs Morgan had proven a great comfort over the course of the illness; they couldn't have managed without her.

"Off with you then, enjoy the rare sunlight." She rushed them out of the house. "Young Freddie says you can have a bit of sweet with your dinner. I've got a Bakewell tart in the oven for us to share."

After what had felt like endless rain, BC had to shield his eyes briefly from the brilliant autumn sun. They strolled slowly along through the gardens, avoiding the bluff and making their way towards the path that led to the beach. Graham had been building his strength with walking and other exercises, coming close to exhausting himself unwisely.

They all knew he would be driven to return to normal. BC didn't have the heart to tell him it might never happen. He would likely always be somewhat marked by his illness.

On their last follow-up with Genevieve, testing had proven the operation had removed all of the cancer. She'd cautioned them on the odds of it returning. Graham hadn't wanted to listen, choosing doggedly to focus on the positives.

Who could blame him?

Not me. Not anyone if they want to keep their teeth from being punched into their throat by Royce Brooks. I won't have anyone diminishing the light returning to his eyes. I've missed it too much.

CHAPTER TWENTY-NINE

GRAHAM

Wanking.

While BC had been the one to break the silence on the subject first, Graham couldn't deny it had been on his mind as well. He missed the sensual connection between them. They'd had a ton of intimacy, but none of it involved sexual anything.

His doctor had promised him all would be normal in that particular arena again. Hair and sex. The two things he viewed as being the pillars of his return to health. He only prayed it happened soon.

Does God care about intercourse?

Shit. Please don't strike me with lightning if you're listening and consider it sacrilege. But honestly, I'd give my left testicle to be able to have the frustration of blue balls, because at least then I'd know I could sodding get it up.

Okay, breathe, Hodson, stop thinking about sex, God, and your knob. Focus on not tumbling head over heels off the side of the cliff.

"I want to get another tattoo." Graham tucked his hands into the pockets on his new jumper. He peered down the path leading to the beach. His goal since returning to the inn after the operation had been to make it down to the shore. "Maybe something to symbolise coming through the other side of this foggy nightmare?"

"What tattoo?" BC placed a hand at his back when he slipped on the gravel. "Think we can manage a little further?"

Shaking his head, Graham meandered carefully away from the rock-covered trail. He didn't think today would be the day his feet touched the sand. Making it down was one thing, but no way could he climb his way back up the hill.

"Let's go around by the cliff instead." Graham kicked absently at a large shell someone had dropped on the path. "My dad told me about this Latin phrase that he wrote on a piece of paper and pinned to the wall in his study. *Non est ad astra mollis e terris via.* He said it helped him feel less— afraid for him."

"My Latin's a bit rusty."

"I think the loose translation is: there is no easy way from the earth to the stars." He pulled his left hand out of his pocket, shoving up the sleeves of both his cardigan and the shirt underneath it. "It would look brilliant with the words wrapped around an old compass, maybe on my bicep."

"How about I book an appointment for us with my tattoo artist in London? You haven't been anywhere but here or Plymouth in what must feel like decades to you." BC had a gleam in his eye that spoke of plans already in motion. "How about it? Are you up for a long jaunt, Ginger Spice?"

"After my chemo." Graham wanted to treat the tattoo as a gift to himself for not giving up. "We've only got four or five weeks to go before I have the last of my treatments. Why don't we go at the beginning of December? I should see if my flat is still standing. It's probably been taken over by dust bunnies."

His apartment was likely perfectly fine. Becca had made monthly visits to check on it for him. She whinged about it not being part of her job description but did it without having been asked.

He and Becca had never had a typical writer/editor relationship. He'd always looked at her as one of his closest friends. They'd even played wingman for each other a few times at clubs and parties.

"I should send Becca a chocolate basket." Graham had to laugh when his random remark caused the man beside him to stumble over a stone. "Having trouble with your sea legs?"

"Why are you sending your editor chocolate?"

"She's obsessed with it?" He shrugged. "It'd be nice to thank her for doing so much for me. I should send Genevieve and Freddie one as well."

"Send Freddie a hot date, he'll appreciate it more. Poor bloke." BC snickered. "He broke up with his last boyfriend."

"The man cheated on him with a family friend. I'd have shoved him off a cliff." Graham had heard all about the relationship disaster from his young nurse during his last visit.

Freddie had been too broken-hearted to hide it. "Don't poke at him again. He doesn't need an old bastard like you reminding him of it."

His heart went out to Freddie. He couldn't ever imagine a friend seducing one of his dates. They might pick at each other, but they'd always stood beside one another.

The nurse had lost not only his first serious boyfriend but a family friend as well. It had been hard on him, and Graham had made Freddie promise to visit more often, not wanting him to sink into a dangerous depression.

"Don't we know someone nice?" BC casually threw out the "we," and it was Graham's turn to stumble over his own feet. "Well? How about the baker?"

"Akash? He's definitely *not* his type." Graham had known Akash for ages. He'd moved from India with his parents at three and made a home for himself in Cornwall. He ran a fusion bakery that combined the flavours of his childhood with Cornish pastries. "Young Freddie needs someone a bit—stronger."

"Rugby strong?"

"Of a sort." Graham wouldn't stroke the overly large ego of the man beside him any more than necessary. "I'll have Francis bug Caddock to see if any of his friends are single and interested in dating."

"Is this the shit we're doing now? Walking and setting people up on dates?" BC slung his arm around Graham's shoulders. "It's rather a *couple* thing to do, isn't it?"

"Shut up."

It was. And it was nice. He didn't have to admit it to BC, though.

CHAPTER THIRTY

BC

October and November flew by quickly, something all the occupants of the Fisherman's Refuge found themselves happy about. By the first day of December, chemotherapy had officially become a thing of the past, with Graham being found free of cancer cells.

It could come back. Genevieve had reiterated her warnings about keeping up with his diet plans and scheduled appointments, but her overall outlook for him was positive. She'd been adamant in her belief he would continue to make a full recovery and live a long, happy life.

The news had made both of them weak at the knees with relief. BC had sat in the chair, stunned, clutching Graham's hand so tightly that it probably hurt. He didn't seem to mind as he clung right back.

Plans were immediately made to take a holiday, of sorts, to London. Becca was ecstatic with the news and promised the flat was more than ready for visitors. She'd even have her part-time housekeeper stop by to spiff it up a bit to welcome them.

Rupert had driven down earlier to bring clothes for his brother. Graham had lost a significant amount of weight from his illness and the treatments to cure it. He had slowly been regaining it, but his trousers practically fell off him without a tight belt to stop them.

The clothes had, thankfully, been purchased by Francis and Joanne, not by Rupert who would've used the opportunity to force his brother into something embarrassing. They'd only gotten a few jeans, shirts, and other essentials. Graham fully believed he would return to his former state, so buying a full wardrobe would've been pointless and a waste of money.

"Rupert snuck one in anyway." Graham held up a bright pink T-shirt with passport stamps all over it. "I love the stamps. Not sure the colour works with my hair. Stupid plonker. This is revenge for the Christmas a few years ago when I shipped him fossilized animal dung for a present. He didn't appreciate it nearly as much as I did."

"Vicious."

Graham grinned mischievously at him. "Rupert and I would fight to the death with each other, but I'll be damned if we don't also tease the bloody shit out of one another at the same time."

"Aren't all siblings complex relations?" BC had no siblings and hadn't ever truly been close with much of his family, extended or immediate. His close relationships outside of romance had been with friends or rugby teammates. He'd always been jealous of close siblings like the Hodsons who made him wonder what he'd missed out on growing up. "Will Rupert and Joanne be meeting us in London at all for the holidays?"

"Not bloody likely. Rupert hates London—or Joanne does, and he agrees with her. I thought we'd be back in Cornwall for Christmas." Graham paused in packing his bag for their journey. "Don't be an arse and change it on me at the last minute. My parents would kill me for missing Boxing Day with them."

"Two weeks in London, last two of December in Cornwall," BC promised.

The flat had already been decorated by Becca. She'd sent a last-minute text message to BC to let him know the tree had gone up. He had no doubts it would be the picture of Christmas joy when they arrived.

Everyone who knew Graham had resolved to make the holidays bright and special for him. It occurred to him that they were all using it as an excuse to soothe their nerves after his brush with death. They'd learnt a lesson about how short life could be.

Knowing Graham as he did, the man wouldn't put up with being smothered with anything, particularly over-the-top holiday nonsense for long. BC planned to do his own part to keep things from getting to be too much for him. He wouldn't be singing carols on Christmas Eve, if only to save everyone's eardrums.

The one plan BC had made was with his tattoo artist. He wanted it to be part of his gift to Graham. The other portion being his intention to get the same Latin phrase inked in the same place.

Romantic? Yes.

Soppy as shit? Definitely.

Do I care? Not a bloody chance.

"My mother wants us to go to the Christmas service at her church." Graham glanced up from his mobile with such a grimace that BC had to laugh at him. "Laugh it up, you numpty, but you'll be going with me if I'm forced into it."

"Shit."

"There'll be free food. The village always has a grand spread to celebrate the birth of 'wee baby Jesus.'" Graham sounded as if he were mimicking someone. He chuckled when BC raised an eyebrow at him in confusion. "My nan talked of the wee baby non-stop through the whole of December. She thankfully had plenty of mince pies to make up for it."

While Graham continued sharing stories of holidays long past, BC returned to packing up his own clothes for their trip. He had his Roadster all geared up and ready. It wouldn't be a Range Rover, but he always felt the larger the vehicle, the more a bloke was compensating, something he'd told Caddock on many occasions.

"Oi?" Graham whacked him on the head with a pair of socks. "I've been ready for hours."

"Hours?" BC raised an eyebrow.

"Maybe twenty minutes." He shrugged.

"Twenty?"

"All right, all right, five," Graham admitted. "Same difference. Get your arse ready. London waits for no man."

"Waits for the Queen."

"Like I said, London waits for no man." He poked BC on the arm.

BC shook his head at the almost giddy energy coming from the redhead. "You've missed traveling, haven't you?"

"Would you miss oxygen if you suddenly couldn't breathe? I don't wander because I've no sodding home. I do it because it's always been in my blood." Graham dropped on the edge of the bed with a groan. "It's the itch I can bloody scratch."

"So, you've missed it then?"

"To quote a friend, 'you're a knobheaded wanker.'"

The six-hour journey to London went brilliantly. Graham had him stopping every thirty minutes or so to take photos. BC found himself getting stupidly misty-eyed at the pure normalcy of the moment.

Each pause in travel added minutes to the overall length of the trip. The massive smile plastered on Graham's face made it impossible for BC to be annoyed by continuous delays. He'd missed the air of excitement and adventure in his wanderer.

Their route to London had avoided the motorway almost entirely until they'd left Cornwall. BC had known Graham would enjoy a more scenic view than the A38. Standing on the beach in Branscombe, he knew it had been the right decision.

They stood together, looking over the wild winter sea. BC couldn't resist catching Graham by the front of his jumper

and dragging him closer. He indulged his hunger for a taste—
their first less-than-innocent kiss in ages.

"*Judas Priest.* I've missed this." BC flicked his tongue
across those slightly swollen lips, diving in for another
bruising kiss. He reached up to carefully readjust Graham's
hat, which he'd dislodged slightly. "Think we can make it to
London before midnight?"

"Is that a hint?"

BC chuckled when Graham nipped at his bottom lip in
retaliation for his nod. "Get your arse to the Roadster. I'll die
of starvation if this four-hour drive takes us ten because of
your pissing away the time."

CHAPTER THIRTY-ONE

His flat had not only been thoroughly cleaned but decorated both tastefully and exquisitely for the season. Faerie lights had been strung across the ceilings of each room, including the kitchen. A tree sat in one corner of his den with the most brilliant travel-themed baubles on it, along with silver tinsel and lights. Candles and holly covered the mantle over his fireplace, creating the complete picture of Christmas.

Becca had certainly outdone herself. Music and presents were the only things missing to complete the scene, and maybe a bit of snow outside. Graham should've known she would go all out to make his homecoming special.

Scratching the growing fuzz on his head, Graham dislodged his knit hat. He caught it and tossed it over to a nearby shelf. Losing his hair had felt like the worst part of chemotherapy, but growing it back wasn't much better thus far.

BC stepped up behind him and ran his own fingers across Graham's scalp. "You look like a boiled egg with a red five o'clock shadow."

"Bastard." Graham scowled at the man who didn't have much more hair on his own head. His glare faded quickly when a yawn overtook him. "You don't look much better."

The six hours of driving, walking, and photographing had worn Graham out. The energy almost visibly evaporated from him. It didn't surprise him when BC picked up on it, not so subtly guiding him towards the bedroom.

"Oi. I know the way, it is my flat. I don't require direction to my own bedroom." Graham swatted absently at the hands on his back. "You'll end up propelling me through a wall if you're not careful."

Shucking off his boots, socks, and jeans, Graham crawled onto his bed, relishing being in familiar territory for once. *Home.* Odd how never before had he actually missed his place. He even clung to his old duvet like a friend who'd been gone for ages.

It had been handwoven in a village in Guatemala. He'd been backpacking through the country and met a sixty-two-year-old woman who made them. He found sitting to watch her work utterly fascinating.

She'd ended up being the subject of his first-ever extended feature with the magazine. The elderly woman still kept in contact with him; her grandchildren would email him on her behalf at least once a year. He'd always intended to return but had yet to have the chance.

The duvet would always be a treasured possession. He had it carefully and professionally laundered every so often. His worst fear would've been ruining it in the wash himself, not that he usually gave a fig about linens.

Hell, my sheets had holes at the corners until Becca forced new ones on me.

"Nap time?" BC collapsed on the bed beside him after toeing off his trainers. He squashed up next to Graham on the double mattress. "My feet are dangling off the edge."

"Tall wanker."

"I'd love to wank something."

"Pervert." Graham chuckled tiredly.

"Sleep. We've a tattoo appointment set up at New Wave Tattoo. Lal Hardy, the owner, did most of my ink, most of the ones for the national team come to think of it. He'll see us in the afternoon." BC looped an arm around him to drag him closer. "You certain you're up for it? I know Genevieve and Freddie both said you'd be fine, but we can put it off another week or two. We'll be in London until mid-December."

"What other things have you planned?" Graham twisted around to face him. He'd been overhearing whispered conversations while BC was on his mobile. "Well? What've you been up to?"

"You know Tens, right?"

Tens?

Ahh, Tens.

Taine Afoa, a rather bloody massive rugby player, originally from Samoa, who'd played for the English team with BC and Caddock. He'd become a legend in the game. Graham knew the man through his brother, who'd helped him find a house in Fowey a few months ago.

"Didn't he move out of London?"

"His girlfriend is an event coordinator. She might've given me a hand with a few ideas." BC blushed a bit, which made Graham laugh. "Oh, shut up and take a nap."

Their nap went a tad longer than intended. Graham awoke groggily around midnight to discover they'd slept through dinner. He considered dropping back off but remembered that missing meals wouldn't do his recovery any favours, so he grabbed a pillow to swat BC in the face until he shot up in bed.

"Oh good, you're up." Graham reclined on the pillow left behind him. "We missed dinner. Are you hungry? I've got to eat to take the vitamins. *Shit.* I didn't think to look in the cabinets or fridge. Think we can get a takeaway at this hour?"

Clad in only boxers and T-shirts, they stumbled down the hall towards the kitchen. Graham kicked at BC's heels, causing the larger man to trip more than once in the process. They giggled giddily by the time they made it to the refrigerator.

"Ahh, Becca handled this as well." Graham grabbed a note resting on top of a number of prepared meals. "Or rather, Freddie apparently didn't want to risk me straying from my diet plan, so he had a local chef make up all of this for me. You, apparently, are supposed to starve in the process."

BC shoved him head first into the fridge only to roar with laughter when Graham came out again with a muffin in his mouth. "Got any more of those?"

They managed to put together a decent midnight spread to nosh on while plotting out their schedule for the rest of the week. Graham needled BC for hints about the secret plans to no avail. He was told to "wait and see," something he didn't do overly well.

Popping a couple grapes into his mouth, Graham flicked through the text messages on his mobile. He'd missed a few while they rested. Becca, Rupert, and Francis had all sent one wanting to know if they'd arrived safely in the city.

Graham sent a short "yes" to the first two, but a more detailed one to Francis. He needed a favour from his old friend. Christmas, after all, was upon them, and presents would need to be purchased.

An idea had been floating around in his mind for a few weeks on what to get for BC. An upcoming auction was supposedly offering Monty Python memorabilia. Something there was sure to make a perfect gift.

Of everyone he knew, Francis would be the best at handling an auction, getting the best price and keeping it anonymous. He perused the list of items curiously. The script and on-set photo collection looked particularly intriguing.

"What *are* you up to over here?" BC tried to read over his shoulder, but Graham elbowed him in the stomach. He coughed loudly and exaggeratedly. "Try not to break my rib, you numpty."

"Don't shove your nose into my business."

"I'll shove something somewhere."

Graham easily dodged the fingers reaching out to

tickle him. He used the moment to set his phone back on the kitchen counter where he'd left it before they napped. "The note says we've got a breakfast booked at Balthazar in the morning."

"Fancy."

"Rather go to the Regency Café, less posh and more substance." Graham hadn't yet been able to stomach heavier food, but Genevieve had given him permission to attempt at least a bit more normal stuff in his diet. "We'll do the swanky stuff tomorrow since Becca went to the trouble of booking a table for us. The rest of the trip though we'll eat our way—not theirs."

"Our way?" BC always had the soppiest smile when Graham said we or our. "It sounds perfect. We could set a budget each day and see how cheaply we can eat in London, maybe try all those hidden places only cabbies know about."

"An adventure?"

"A Christmas adventure." BC snagged a stray bit of mistletoe dangling from the ceiling and held it over Graham's head. "Give us a kiss?"

"I'll give you a Scottish one if you don't stop hitting me in the head with that bunch of twigs." He had to duck his head to avoid the mistletoe. He chuckled when BC lowered it to dangle in front of his boxers. "I'm not quite ready for you to drop your pants."

BC tossed the mistletoe over his head blindly. "Ah well, it's not like we don't have all the time in the world."

"We do, now." Graham had taken months for it to truly sink in that the operation had been a success. "So, adventure now, and sex later?"

"Brilliant."

The posh restaurant had been as advertised—brilliant food, but too buttoned-up for them. Nothing either of them would've wanted to write home about or visit again. It seemed more geared towards suited-up toffs having business meetings.

As Graham progressed further into his recovery, he had become almost obsessed with food. It might've been caused by having to go from liquid diet to soft food to intravenous feeding and back again. He wondered if it would alter his writing.

Travel writer to food writer? It doesn't sound completely daft.

They'd gone from Balthazar to the tattoo shop, using the cab ride across the city to plan out the rest of their afternoon. The ink would take several hours, leaving plenty of time to start their exploration of the hidden parts of London. *Maybe not hidden, that's a bit dramatic. More non-tourist London. Oh, I'm a bloody ponce now. Shut up, Graham, shut up.*

"Stop talking to yourself." BC smirked knowingly at him.

Graham tilted his mobile so BC could read it. "Becca wants me to write about London restaurants—the popular and unknown alike."

"Genevieve approved?"

"I'll have to be careful." Graham's eyes had a gleam of excitement in them, one that had been missing for months. "Smaller portions, less greasy options. I can manage it. How about you? You up for it?"

"I'm always up for it." He grinned cheekily.

"*Idiot.*"

"Where we going first?"

"Dishoom."

"Bless you."

Graham snorted loudly, as did their cab driver. "It's a restaurant, you plonker, one of my favourites. They've got this bacon naan roll. It's life-changing."

"A naan roll?"

They pulled up outside of the tattoo shop, cutting off their conversation. BC had originally intended to drive himself, but being stuck in London traffic would've made them completely bonkers. They'd opted for using cabs instead.

Graham was confused when they were both led to chairs at the shop to get inked. He blushed, went misty-eyed, and then got angry at his own reaction when he realised BC would be getting the same tattoo. They sat across from each other, grimacing as the needles started.

Five hours getting tattooed did Graham in utterly. They forwent Dishoom to return to his flat. The restaurant wouldn't be going anywhere.

They had time.

When they finally arrived at his place, BC had to practically carry him up the stairs to his front door. Graham crawled on the sofa and almost curled up on his side. He was snoring before his head fully rested on one of the couch cushions.

***

"Bloody hell." Graham shot up out of sleep, completely out of breath and a bit in shock. He rubbed his arm with a wince. Good news? He hadn't rested on the freshly inked skin. Bad news? It was on the arm where he received his injections. "I dreamt Alan Rickman tattooed a portrait of his character from *Die Hard* on my arse."

Because of the chemotherapy and diet restrictions, Graham had been getting frequent vitamin shots to boost his immune system. It was critical to avoid simple illnesses like the flu during the winter months. His recovery could be permanently slowed at this critical juncture.

"Kinky, also bizarre." BC grinned at him. "On that *fascinating* note, I'm half-starved. Are you hungry?"

"Not overly." Graham shrugged.

"You have to eat." He tried his best never to nag at him about food. "Let's see what the chef's cooked up for us."

"Might as well eat."

CHAPTER THIRTY-TWO

BC

The following morning saw the two men awake with sore biceps. They checked their tattoos, removing the bandages before first washing, then drying, and finally applying the ointment the artist had given them. BC had gingerly traced the lines of the compass on his new ink while staring at it in the mirror.

Non est ad astra mollis e terris via.

There is no easy way from earth to the stars.

It fit Graham so perfectly. No matter what happened between them now, they would both always have a reminder of their time together slogging through the hell of cancer. The art on their arms held a remarkable poignancy.

"You keep thinking so hard, and you're going to break something." Graham flicked one of the used flannels at him.

"What do you say to stretching the horizon of your taste buds? Dishoom for breakfast?"

Bacon naan rolls turned out to be far tastier than imagined. The Kejriwal wasn't half-bad either—couldn't spell it, but definitely managed to eat two plates of the fried eggs on chilli cheese toast. They made their way through a surprising number of dishes together because it seemed the key to Graham's appetite was expanding his choices.

They also tried out some of the tea flavours on offer. BC found his favourite three things blended in their chai experiment. The chocolate chai melded spices with dark chocolate and he fell immediately in lust with it, much to Graham's amusement if his snickering behind his own drink were anything to go by.

When they'd made the decision to explore London, BC had contacted several friends for ideas. One of them, a baker originally from Cornwall who had been introduced to him by Jack, suggested one of the baking courses at Bread Ahead. They'd managed to weasel their way into a mince pie workshop.

Full up on their spiced breakfast, the two men made their way to the school slash bakery for their mid-morning course. Three hours to learn how to create the best mince pies. *Ten quid says we eat more than we actually bake.* A glance around the room told him not many men took advantage of the lessons.

Three hours.

Three. Hours.

Three. Sodding. Hours.

In the scope of the morning, BC found himself covered in flour, sugar, and eggs. Butter wound up in his hair. His trainers were completely ruined with a combination of all of the above.

On the plus side, as two attractive and fit men in a room with mostly women of all ages, they'd ended up with arms full of mince pies. Graham had gotten kisses from all of them, particularly when they learnt about his recovery from cancer after one of the ladies turned out to be an aunt of Freddie's. They'd been invited over for tea and scones later in the week.

How precisely does one turn down a seventy-six-year-old?

One doesn't, particularly when she was wearing a bright red Santa jumper and a hat.

Stuffed up on mince pies, BC had the idea to head to one of the Christmas markets around the city. *Brilliant.* They didn't so much wander as queue up for the carousel. They hopped on the pastel animals and rode around until the twenty-year-old in charge of the ride kicked them off; apparently, the kiddies deserved a chance to get on it.

BC couldn't help but snicker a bit. "I've never been kicked off a unicorn."

"Naughty, BC." Graham rubbed absently at his lower abdomen, making BC wonder if his stomach had started to hurt him. "Enough with the look, I'm fine."

"You sure?" He didn't think the man quite appeared completely all right. "Why don't we go to your place for a few hours to rest?"

"I don't need a sodding nap. I'm not a child," Graham

snapped at him. He pinched the bridge of his nose, breathing heavily while his other hand continued to massage his stomach. "I hate this. Hate it. I'm glad the cancer's gone, not like I wanted to die. Recovery is almost as shit, though. The operation was ages ago. I should be *fine*. Shit."

"Ages ago?" He reached out to rest his hands on the ginger's tense shoulders. "A couple of months aren't quite what I would consider the distant past. Has your memory gone to shit with everything else?"

"Plonker."

"Me?" BC shook him by the shoulders gently. "I'm not the one having a fit over a nap. You sure you're not a toddler?"

The comment earned him an elbow in the side. He wasn't surprised when they did end up making their way to the flat. Nor was it a shock when the still recovering man slipped under the covers on the bed to nap for several hours.

Settling down to read yet another novel, BC sipped tea and flipped pages without reading a word. He had a problem. *A big one.* He had an utterly massive issue with no clue how to handle it.

I am in love.

Graham is in love with me.

Neither of us is emotionally mature enough to want to discuss this beyond our initial potentially death bed confession.

So, essentially, we're completely buggered and not in the fun way.

"You're going to get wrinkles."

BC swatted away at the fingers playing with his forehead.

"Done napping?"

"What's got you looking like an old man?" Graham perched on the arm of the chair. "C'mon then, I've spilled my secrets to you. What have you been sniffing?"

"Sounds dirtier and more perverse every time you say it."

"*Brilliant.*"

BC shoved him off the chair and grinned down at him. "So—we're in love."

Graham stayed on the floor, blinking up at him with confusion clear in his eyes. "Right."

"Aren't we?"

"*Right.*" Graham dragged the word out slowly.

"We're shit at this." BC decided to state the obvious.

Graham shuffled backwards until he could lean against the edge of the couch. "Total shit. We've had this conversation already, you plonker."

"I'm old. Allow me some much-needed clarification." He tried to press him for a clear answer.

"Yes, Prime Minister." Graham saluted.

"Numpty." BC kicked the bottom of his foot. "Are we in a relationship?"

"A shit one, but yes."

"Good." BC scratched the side of his jaw for a minute. "*Judas Priest.* Does this mean I have to get you a present?"

"Yes. A good one, as well." Graham nodded with feigned seriousness.

"Needy bastard."

CHAPTER THIRTY-THREE

GRAHAM

Beef pho from Mien Tay in Battersea warmed their stomachs perfectly. They'd ventured out after their attempt to cook the meal put together for them by the chef ended in a kitchen fire. *Fire bad.* His hob would need serious cleaning after the smoke cleared out—a problem for another day.

Jotting down notes in his travel journal, Graham made sure to cover every detail of their food adventure. He'd based his life in London ever since university, but never truly bothered with what could be found in the city. Becca had already sent him a massive list of places to keep him busy; she wasn't usually quite so transparent.

They'd frittered the rest of their day away. Now Graham sat on the couch in his living room at four in the morning while BC slept soundly down the hall. He'd been reading through the many emails from his treatment team multiple times, wanting to ensure he'd understood everything.

His frustration had boiled over earlier as a direct result of some of these messages. They'd all warned him about fatigue continuing to be a problem for what could be a potentially prolonged period up to several years post-surgery. *Just sodding brilliant.* If it weren't enough to be a swooning mess, he'd also have to watch carefully for any latent side effects from both the operation and chemotherapy.

Several of the comments in the emails stood out to him. "You may experience trouble in regards to sexual function." Translation? *Good luck trying to wank, you tosser.* His other particular favourite had been warnings on his memory being affected. He found added cautions on energy levels equally bemusing and distressing.

Even if I can get it up, I'll be too bloody tired to use it.

Chemotherapy might've saved his life, but down the road, it could cause issues with his heart, lungs, or give him another form of cancer. He couldn't help wonder if the cure had been worse than the sickness. *Don't be daft.* It wasn't. A lifetime of looking out for potential side effects was better than being six feet under.

The general consensus from both his doctor and family seemed to agree on travelling being ill-advised. He wouldn't be going beyond British borders for at least a year, maybe even longer. He wanted to sob uncontrollably about it. No flying? No exotic locations? No hiking up little-known trails?

Tragic.

Genevieve wanted him close enough for follow-up appointments. She also worried about him overdoing it. Exhaustion could still do him serious harm even after he felt at full strength.

Full strength?

I just want a bloody orgasm. Well, not bloody, but—bugger.

"Oi! Ginger Spice." BC lumbered loudly down the hall, banging into the bookshelf and wall from the sounds of the thuds. "Come to bed. It's freezing in your bedroom. Haven't you heard of hypothermia? Did you have to steal the damn blanket?"

"It's not that cold."

"I'm freezing my bollocks off." BC threw himself on the sofa beside Graham, sending it skidding across the small gap to bump against the wall. He grabbed the smaller man and dragged him over on his lap along with the aforementioned blanket. "What're you doing up at this time?"

Graham stretched his legs out along the cushions. "Picturing the future."

"Aliens and space travel and shit?"

"No, you daft arse, my future, not the distant one from movies." He rolled his eyes at the ridiculous comment but had to chuckle with him. "Becca's trying to distract me from leaving the country by reassigning me to the London section of the travel magazine—food and entertainment, to be more specific."

"I'm in."

"You're in what?" Graham asked blankly.

BC lifted a hand to pretend to check him over for a fever.

"You're not usually this slow. Or would you rather wander around the city by yourself?"

"And you're calling me dim?" He reached under the man's T-shirt to tweak one of his nipples. "Of course I don't want to go by myself. There's not much worse than sitting in a restaurant on my own with no one to laugh at my brilliant jokes."

"Great. Crisis averted. Can we get some sleep now?" BC stood up with Graham still in his lap and managed to heft him awkwardly over his shoulder to lug him down the hall. Graham took advantage of the situation to reacquaint himself with the attractive arse practically shoved in his face. They ended up collapsing on the bed laughing hysterically. "Night night, Ginger Spice."

"Sleep tight, book sniffer."

They lay in silence for almost ten minutes.

"I'm hungry."

"I could eat." Graham sat up with his back resting against the headboard. "Beans on toast?"

"Can your kitchen handle another one of our attempts to cook?" BC rolled over until his head rested on Graham's thigh. "Your neighbours might not appreciate an early morning evacuation. Think anyone delivers at this time?"

"I've a much better idea."

"Oh?"

"Definitely. Oh, and by the way, you plonker, we wouldn't have set the kitchen on fire if you hadn't been throwing shit at me." Graham flicked him on the ear. "Up you get."

"Me? You started it." BC twisted his head to bite the younger man on the thigh. "So, where are we off to for breakfast?"

"You'll see."

At five in the morning, they buckled up in the Roadster and made a mad dash across the city. Graham's directions got them lost—twice. They eventually ended up outside one of the few twenty-four-hour breakfast spots he knew about in London.

"Here?"

"Scared, Brooks?"

"No more Harry Potter memes for you." BC started to get out of the vehicle but stopped when Graham reached out for his arm. "Problem?"

"Not exactly." Graham moved his hand up to wrap around the former rugby player's thick neck. *I. Want. A. Sodding. Snog.* He'd get one, as well. "Come here."

Their mouths touched hesitantly at first, gently reacquainting themselves with each other. Tongues barely flicked out against lips. They breathed in one another with shaky, airy exhales.

Graham grasped at BC desperately to keep him from pulling away, having his first flash of true arousal in months. "Oh, thank God, my boy still works."

BC started to respond only to turn his head when a sharp bang sounded on the driver-side window. It spooked both of them. He lowered the window and froze at the uniformed officer frowning at them disapprovingly. "How can I help, sir?"

"Keep it in your pants, lads. All right? I'll not have you doing all sorts of things on my street." The officer tapped his hand against the door. "Move along, or get yourselves inside."

"Yes, of course." BC waited until the man had moved on to roll up the window. He met Graham's eyes, who immediately lost his battle with laughter. "Brilliant plan, Ginger Spice. Did you want your breakfast with a side of arrest?"

Graham ignored him completely, focusing on the tent in his trousers. He poked at it gently. "I missed you."

"*Daft idiot.*"

CHAPTER THIRTY-FOUR

BC

Six days into their trip to the city, BC had begun to grow increasingly concerned about Graham. The younger man had become driven by discovering sex wouldn't be a thing of the past. He'd pushed himself to dangerous levels of exhaustion while exploring London.

He could understand. Life had changed too drastically. It was obvious Graham wanted everything to return to the way it had been.

Before. Cancer.

After a day spent touring one market after the other, Graham had insisted on immediately heading out in the evening to a comedy club. Despite his obviously flagging energy levels, he'd refused any attempt to put it off. They could find tickets for another night, but he wasn't interested.

He wanted to go tonight. So they went. He swooned into his pudding in the middle of the fourth comedian's act.

Sodding swooned.

After a humiliating evening in the hospital, Graham had finally been willing to agree to return to a more sedate pace. He could do more than during treatment, but definitely not to the point of fainting into spotted dick. BC had gone out of his way to take the mickey over that pertinent fact.

It had been an embarrassing lesson to learn. Their moods had plummeted considerably after returning to the flat from the hospital. Graham had obviously decided to hole up and soothe his wounded pride.

The one great shame had been no more kissing. BC had been enjoying their return to intimacy. He hadn't expected it to be derailed so soon, and couldn't help hoping it would continue once the gloomy mood had been shaken off.

Days continued to pass, until they had only one left in London before the scheduled trip back to Cornwall. The cloud of doom had yet to lift from the flat. The time had definitely come to do something about it.

Operation Cheer the Ginger is a go.

A short text message to Becca had a delivery of several DVDs of comedic holiday specials, a mountain of Christmas biscuits, and the ingredients to make boozed-up hot chocolate arriving within an hour. The woman could work miracles. He had no doubts she could run the entire nation if given the chance.

The operation didn't go off completely without a hitch. Graham hadn't wanted to move out of bed. BC had forced the issue, wrapping the man up in a blanket and lugging him down the hallway into the living room to dump him on the couch.

"You sodding arse." Graham stumbled out of the blanket to launch himself at BC. "Stop tickling me."

"Why?" BC used his superior strength to pin Graham's arms to his sides with one arm while his other hand reached out to feather along his side. "Act like a toddler, get teased like one."

The brief spurt of energy disappeared quickly, leaving Graham worn out and easy to shift onto the couch. He did manage a wry chuckle that BC imagined was directed at both of them. They'd had their first fight.

A tickle one, but a fight all the same.

"Eat a gingerbread man and shut it." BC tossed one of the biscuits across the room. "Mr Bean does Christmas?"

"Is that really the title?" Graham leaned forward to get a closer look at the DVD case. "So, not the actual name, but honestly, they did a Mr Bean Christmas special?"

"When in Rome."

"What?"

"No idea." BC decided to stop talking nonsense and get on with the cheering up. "Rowan Atkinson, ginger biscuits, and hot chocolate. Merry Christmas to us."

"Happy Christmas—two weeks early—you utter imbecile."

"One week." BC grinned.

After good-natured grumbling, they settled down on the couch together. They yanked the blanket back and forth until finally draping it over both of them. Graham drifted off to sleep thirty minutes into the special.

Typical.

BC worked his way through all the biscuits. He tried to stretch his arm out to get a drink and ended up knocking Graham to the floor. *Shit.* They stared at each other and shared a laugh.

"You ate all the biscuits." Graham glared at the now empty plate. "Who eats all the sodding biscuits?"

"I'm a growing lad."

"You're an overgrown fuckwit."

"*Oi.*" BC grabbed a cushion from the couch to swat Graham in the head. "I left the shortbread."

"Only because you couldn't reach it."

"Maybe."

"Growing lad, my arse."

The plate of shortbread disappeared equally quickly. They made short work of all the treats. It left them groaning on the floor with tummy aches and reminded BC a bit too much of candy binges with his schoolmates in his youth.

Graham rummaged through the remnants of the delivery from Becca, obviously looking for something. He held up a massive tube of Smarties triumphantly. "Yes!"

BC shook his head in bemusement when green eyes watched him suspiciously. "What's your damage now?"

"Hands off the Smarties." Graham shuffled across the floor away from him with the tube clutched to his chest. "My precious."

"Keep them." BC grabbed another one of the DVDs.

"You realise we're going to have to pack up tonight, so don't get too hopped up on sugar. Your brother's expecting us for supper tomorrow night."

"Shit."

"He's your twin."

"Double shit."

BC snorted. "Careful with all the sugar, don't want to cause any problems with your shrunken insides."

"You laugh. He'll have heard about my fainting and make jokes all night." Graham lifted the tube of sweets to funnel some into his mouth, crunching through them loudly. "Joanne's a brilliant cook, but I'm not sure it's worth the pain and suffering about to be heaped on me."

"Suffering?" BC couldn't stop his eyebrows from lifting up in disbelief. "I've seen you give as good as you get from Rupert. Never mind you've been through hell and back, surely a night with your twin doesn't compare."

"I'm not at my fighting weight."

"Call in sick." BC shrugged.

"Use the cancer card?" Graham dumped the last of the sweets in his mouth. "Might as well. It won't work forever. I could tell the plonker I'm too delicate for any sort of upset."

"Delicate? You?" He couldn't imagine the strong, but admittedly still slightly frail man ever being considered fragile. "You're not made of glass."

"You sure? I sodding swooned."

"You fainted because you were too bloody stubborn to listen to Genevieve, Freddie, and me when we said you shouldn't try to do too much too soon." BC refused to give the dose of honesty with a drop of sugar. Graham had to hear the unvarnished truth. "Recovery takes time. You had surgery and chemo. Your body has been through the shit cycle of life. Give it time."

"Don't misquote the doctor," Graham muttered petulantly. "I couldn't help myself. It felt too damn good to seem normal. Running around, taking photos, eating amazing food. I didn't want to lose any of the experience because of a nap."

"Never said stop, only slow yourself down." BC scooted over to drop a hand on Graham's shoulder. "Think of it as a forced stay in the sin bin. Sit on your arse for a bit, and then go back to having a good time."

"Naughty boys go to the sin bin."

"Oi, none of that, not when I'm not allowed to bugger you into the floor."

"Just the floor?"

BC reached down to adjust the hardening in his jeans, relieving the sudden pressure. "Bastard. Teasing me when I can't do anything about it."

"Think of it as a forced stay in the sin bin," Graham parroted back to him.

He stroked himself through his jeans with a few casual tugs. "Wanker."

"Me?" Graham stared pointedly at BC's moving fingers. "I think the proof is in the pudding."

BC paused to frown at him. "The proof is in the pudding? What?"

As they laughingly returned to the telly, BC found his

mind drawn to other things. He'd been sexually frustrated for ages. It almost felt disloyal to even attempt to get off without Graham.

"BC?"

He nearly fell off the couch when fingers dropped on his crotch. "You have my full attention."

"I could—"

"No, not until we're both ready."

"You sure? I wouldn't be such a noble shit about it." Graham squeezed once before removing his hand.

"You would."

"Not likely."

He would. BC had no doubts.

CHAPTER THIRTY-FIVE

GRAHAM

Dinner at his twin's place had started out as an awkward disaster. His sister-in-law could usually be relied upon to be the intelligent and sensible one in her marriage, but Joanne had almost smothered him with comfort while Rupert practically strained a muscle in his attempt to not laugh at his brother or tease him.

Sympathy, Graham had learned, could be incredibly exhausting. Well-intentioned friends and family would dump their tears and worries on his shoulders and leave feeling like they'd done him good. He didn't want it—none of the emotional vomit from them helped him.

What do I want?

Everyone to act normal—as much as they're able.

"Surprised you didn't invite Francis, Caddock, and

their little Devlin." Graham tried to bridge the gap of yet another awkward silence. "Were they busy?"

He knew his brother and sister-in-law dined at least once a week with the married couple and their adopted son. Devlin was the only child of Caddock's brother who had died tragically, leaving the boy to his elder sibling. The little devil was a bright spark of life who cheered everyone around him up.

Joanne took Rupert's hand when he couldn't speak. "We didn't want to overwhelm you."

Graham mouthed "overwhelm" to BC, who shrugged, appearing equally befuddled. "How would three additional guests, who I happen to know well, be too much for me?"

"You...." Rupert sounded as though his throat had clogged with tears.

Oh, for God's sake.

Graham stood up suddenly, and BC's hand went out to prevent his chair from clattering to the floor. "I had cancer. The big sodding *C*. I'm not dead. I'm tired. I'm particularly tired of everyone acting as if I'd died. Stop. It."

"Right." BC got up and herded him out into the back garden. He yelled over his shoulder, "Give us a moment if you don't mind."

"Well, shit." Graham dropped down on one of the swings in the set that had been put up for Devlin to play on whenever Joanne babysat for him. "I could've handled that better."

"Probably." BC sat on the other swing. He pushed forward once, the set creaked loudly, and the chain snapped.

It sent him crashing to the ground. "Judas Priest."

"You broke the swing."

"A little help?"

Graham ignored the hand held out to him in a request for assistance. "You broke the swing."

"I'm aware."

"Oi. He broke our swing," Rupert yelled from the house. "He's paying for it. What's a great giant rugby prick doing on a kiddie swing?"

"Swinging," Graham sniped drolly. "We weren't shagging on it—yet."

Rupert's eyes twinkled with familiar mischief. "If you do, make sure you use condoms."

"*Rupert. Hodson.*" Joanne grabbed him by the shirt to drag him into the house. "Honestly."

"See?" Graham nodded his head towards the house where they could see his petite sister-in-law having a go at her husband, who continued to laugh. "Completely normal."

"Wonderful."

Kicking his legs against the grass, Graham swung himself up higher and higher. He enjoyed the wind in his face. *Carefree.* BC stretched out on the ground with his head resting on his arms to stare up at the sky overhead.

"Beautiful night," BC commented idly. "Stars are out. Freezing my bollocks off, but it could be worse."

"Come get your jackets before you turn blue. Idiot twats," Rupert called. "My Joanne has tea ready. She says I should apologise. Says a lot of things. Get your arses inside or put your coats on. I'm not explaining to Mum how you froze your tits off."

Graham reached up to fondle his chest. "Don't have them."

"Twat."

"Twit," Graham retorted. "Give us a second, Rupert."

"Suit yourselves."

"You wanted normal." BC got to his feet and yanked Graham off the swing. "Let's get inside for tea."

After a much more comfortable pudding and tea, they made their excuses and left for Torpoint. It was a relief to drive up to the inn. No one to bother them aside from Zeus, since Mrs Morgan was spending Christmas with her family in the village.

Trudging through the dark hall to BC's room they found Zeus happily ensconced on a pillow on the bed. Graham cheerfully greeted the Yorkie. He ignored the grumbling behind him about "sodding fur getting sodding everywhere."

He sat on the edge of the mattress, petting Zeus absently. It would be Christmas in a little over a week. What would they do to celebrate?

"Want to go to church with me on Christmas Eve?" Graham set Zeus back on his pillow. "Or maybe earlier? When do they have carol services?"

"Not a clue." BC dropped the bag he'd been unpacking. "When was the last time you went to church?"

Graham scratched at the growing stubble on his head. "The wedding? Never been a fan of cassock-clad men lecturing me about life."

"And so?"

He shrugged.

Twice.

How did he explain the sudden desire to make good with whatever higher power had spared him? It sounded ridiculous thinking it, never mind saying the words. He didn't even know what he believed.

"Mrs Morgan will know the service times." BC filled the silence without asking any of those unwanted questions other people would've. "Want to invite anyone else?"

"*No*. I fucking don't."

"All right."

Graham continued to massage his itchy scalp, annoyed with himself for snapping at BC. "Sorry. You don't deserve my temper."

"I can take it." BC grabbed at his sizeable package. "You can make up for it later."

"Arse."

"There as well." BC adjusted himself in his trousers while Graham couldn't help but watch.

"Plonker."

Several days later, on Christmas Eve, they attended an evening mass at St. James Church in Torpoint. Joint choirs had come together for a special event. Mrs Morgan had been delighted at their interest and insisted on bringing them with her. Neither of them could figure out a way to say no to her.

Sitting on an uncomfortable pew for hours listening to the caterwauling of Mrs Morgan felt more like penance than an offering of gratitude. BC snickered quietly beside him whenever she attempted a particularly high note. "The Hallelujah Chorus" had them both biting their lips to avoid roaring with laughter.

"King would've stood up for a whole other reason if he'd heard her," Graham whispered to BC over the cover of yet another round of carols. "Think this is why earplugs were invented?"

BC elbowed him hard in the side. "Shut it."

"Sorry." He wasn't, not even a little.

The best part of the evening had to be the frosted biscuits brought by a local baker, Akash Robinson. He'd come with his mum, who apparently attended St. James's frequently. The Indian-spiced gingerbread had been a fascinating flavour combination.

They'd need more biscuits.

Many. Many. More.

CHAPTER THIRTY-SIX

BC

Christmas dawned—not bright, but grey, frigid, and foggy. BC had to laugh when he spotted the socks hanging from the bedposts, one on either side for each of them. Mrs Morgan had clearly come to visit. He nudged Graham to wake him up.

Nothing.

Slightly harder shove.

Nothing.

Not wanting to chuck the man out of bed, BC grabbed a thread from the blanket and tickled Graham's nose. A hand batted away the teasing thread, but he kept up with it until the redhead finally sat up. His green eyes glared while he struggled through a yawn.

"*Arse.*"

"Happy Christmas." BC pointed towards the stockings.

"Santa paid us a visit."

"Did he look remarkably like an older woman with frizzy grey hair?" Graham accepted the bright red sock tossed to him. He plucked out one of the chocolate bars from it. "Brilliant."

"We've a tree and everything." He'd decorated in the middle of the night after Graham had taken his medicine and fallen into a deep sleep. "Family won't be expecting us until tomorrow, so it's us for the day."

"If you think my brother will miss showing up randomly at some point, you aren't giving him enough credit." Graham tilted up his stocking to dump the contents out on the bed. "Oh, brilliant, she got me condoms."

"She didn't."

Graham held one of the holiday-themed foil wrappers up. "She did."

"Judas. Priest." BC shook his own sock out to find he'd been given lube. "Maybe it wasn't Mrs Morgan?"

"I'm struggling with the image of her purchasing eggnog and mulled wine flavoured rubbers." Graham began shoving the items back into his stocking. "Maybe Rupert paid a visit? Or Caddock? I could see Joanne or Francis insisting on adding the chocolates, tea packets, and other gifts, but caving to their spouses to put in the silly things."

"Wonder if it really tastes of mince pie?" BC grabbed one of the condoms. He held it up to his nose to see if he could pick up any hint of a scent. "Save them. We can experiment."

"Research?"

"In-depth research, of course. Have to be completely thorough." Graham winked at him. He glanced around the room with a confused frown, causing BC to follow his gaze.

"Where's Zeus?"

"It must've been Mrs Morgan. She usually takes him home with her at least once or twice a week. Spoils the furry rodent." BC hopped out of bed, tripping on the blanket draped across his legs. *Okay, BC, get your arse in gear, time to show the ginger a good holiday.* "If it was her, I imagine she's left us breakfast. Hungry?"

"Presents first." Graham retrieved a gift that had apparently been hidden in the wardrobe. "Happy Christmas."

BC shook the large box cautiously, listening to several items sliding around inside. *A book? Several books?* He ripped off the wrapping and tossed it carelessly over his shoulder. He peeked inside before yanking the lid off the package entirely. "How the bloody hell did you get all of this?"

His gift appeared to be a wealth of Monty Python memorabilia. He spotted a signed script along with a massive number of candid photos clearly taken on-set or during rehearsals. It was a treasure trove of memories from his favourite show.

After perusing some hilarious Polaroids, BC set it aside to dig through the boxes around the tree for Graham's gift. It had been a struggle for him to think up something worthwhile. He'd wanted the present to be special—memorable—not a random trinket easily forgotten in a fortnight.

Over the many hours of Graham's recuperation, while the man slept through pain and exhaustion, BC had worked on the project. He'd created a large picture book of his wanderer's travels. It included articles, photos, and other items from the many countries he'd visited.

Once Becca heard about the idea, she'd offered some suggestions along with shipping him a packet of items to include. He'd found a bookmaker through Francis who could create a custom leather-bound masterpiece for him. It had taken a lot of work over the months to finish.

He hadn't honestly thought he had such dedication in him. It had turned out brilliantly. Now all he could do was wait to see if the intended recipient loved it, or laughed him out of the room.

"Well?" BC snapped impatiently. He tapped his fingers while Graham stared at the book, absently flipping through the pages. "Do you hate it? Shit. You think I'm a soppy plonker, don't you? Should've got you something else."

"Breathe, you numpty." Graham traced the lines of a vintage map, one BC had found in his father's library and included at the front. He'd drawn pins to mark all the countries the wanderer had visited. "It's sodding brilliant. How did you find all of this? All my articles and photos. I've kept a journal, you know, but I've never had all my words and adventures put together in a single book. Thank you, BC. I love it. I do. It's probably the best bloody present I've ever been given."

Oh. Good.

Thank God.

"BC?" Graham caught his attention, pulling BC out of his elated thoughts. "If I were soppy, I'd have flowery words of love and gratitude. I'm not, so—thanks, wanker."

BC side-stepped around the foot of the bed and ran his fingers over the growing stubble on Graham's scalp. He bent down to graze his lips against that irresistibly grinning mouth.

"You're welcome, ungrateful bastard."

After a lengthy and languid caressing duel of their tongues, they both had to breathe in gulps of air. BC loomed over Graham, even bent over at the waist. He stood upright, intending to move away, only to freeze in place when fingers grazed across his boxer-covered cock.

He ached, painfully, in his lust for release, had done for days. His arousal hung hot and heavy, even with the devilish fingers dipping inside his pants. "Don't tease me now, Ginger Spice. Not sure I could take it."

The wicked fingers tugged down on the waistband of his boxers. BC's shaft bounced free and swung lightly against Graham's chin. They both chuckled.

Touches. Teases. Licks. It prolonged what would've likely been a short and sudden explosion. BC clutched at the bedpost with one hand while his other guided Graham's bobbing head. He loved the silken lips gliding along his cock. *Best. Fucking. Sensation. In. Existence.* He could sink into that mouth and lose himself forever.

And he did.

The top of the bedpost creaked under the pressure of his tightly squeezing fingers. BC tried to pull away with a warning shout. Graham ignored him, sucking harder and flicking his tongue around.

"Judas Priest. Suck me dry." BC ended up dropping to his knees with a painful crash when his legs went out from under him. He rested his forehead on Graham's leg with a tired but happy sigh. "Merry Christmas. Ready for me to return the favour?"

"Not necessary, not yet." Graham's ears were tinged with pink, a sure sign of embarrassment. "Why don't we see about breakfast?"

BC decided not to exacerbate the situation by drawing attention to Graham's continued difficulties left over from his illness. "Right. Breakfast. We've sorted your protein out already."

Graham choked for a second before laughing hard enough to force him to hold his side. "You kiss your mum with that mouth?"

"I could ask the same." BC lifted his hand to wipe the side of Graham's mouth, not that anything was really there. "Messy, messy lad."

"You utter wanker." Graham punched him lightly on the side of the hip. "Let's get food."

Their instincts proved correct when they found a Christmas breakfast laid out for them on the kitchen table along with a note from Mrs Morgan. It was a simple meal—scones and bacon sarnies, with fruit for Graham, of course. They had tea with it, a special blend for the holidays, one they immediately poured down the sink after a single sip.

"It's like a spiced fruit cake vomited in my mouth." BC grimaced distastefully. He quickly scrounged around in the cupboards to find the regular breakfast tea. He could brew it without setting the inn ablaze, hopefully. "Awful shit. Who thought figgy pudding tea was a good idea?"

"The same evil bastard who made those eggnog and cranberry custard tarts—the ones Joanne forced on us. Vile things." Graham shuddered. "I'm convinced it was Rupert's idea."

They spent a lovely quiet Christmas together. Despite their concerns, no one intruded on the solace of the day. Mrs Morgan brought a meal up for them around lunch. She'd decided to keep Zeus with her, wanting his company, or so she claimed.

As night fell, they bundled up to sit outside and enjoy the unusually clear sky. They had hot tea and a blanket. They had each other.

A perfect end to a perfect Christmas in what had been a not so perfect year.

CHAPTER THIRTY-SEVEN

GRAHAM

Over the course of his travels, Graham had spent New Year's Eve in a variety of interesting places. This year had been no different; invitations had come in from most of their friends and family. The trouble was on every December 31, he ended up surrounded by cheerful revellers in the midst of the party.

It wasn't what he longed for this year. He wanted a moment of reflection. During one of his counselling sessions with Freddie, he'd acknowledged how facing his own mortality continued to affect him emotionally.

Part of his ongoing treatment plan included therapy sessions, a careful diet, and working out. He would follow up with Genevieve once a month until February, and if everything remained clear, it would change to a visit every three months. Cancer had left a permanent mark on him, one that wouldn't be easily or speedily erased.

Christmas had helped. *What a surprise.* They'd visited with both sets of parents. It had gone better than imagined. No rude comments from anyone other than Rupert; his twin could always be counted on to find something to mock—no matter the occasion.

A trait we've always had in common.

What was I thinking about?

Oh, yes, New Year's Eve.

Graham wandered through the inn until he found BC working at the small table in the kitchen. "Oi, book sniffer, what are we doing tonight?"

"Not sniffing books." BC didn't look up from the forms in front of him. "Weren't you in charge of the plans for New Year's?"

Shit.

"Might've forgotten."

"Might have?" BC raised his eyes up to meet Graham's gaze. "Caddock and Francis are throwing a party. He sent me a text message about it earlier. Or we could enjoy our last evening alone at the inn as Mrs Morgan will be returning along with guests."

"Kicking us out, is she?"

He shook his head with a wry chuckle. "Bed and breakfasts only work when people are staying in them who actually pay for the privilege. As we've got my Uncle Davie's old room, we're welcome to remain as long as we wish."

"But?"

"Well." BC rubbed the back of his neck uneasily.

"According to the will, I couldn't sell my stake in the Fisherman's Refuge for a year. It's been in my family for centuries, but I've no interest in running the place. Mrs Morgan would make a better owner. She's already in charge and doing brilliantly."

"What about your family?" Graham went over to the counter to turn on the electric kettle. This would definitely be a conversation that required tea. "The Brookses have always been associated with the inn, haven't they?"

"None of them have said sod all about it since Uncle Davie's death." BC shrugged. He gestured carelessly towards the piled up papers around him. "Even handing over the daily management to her, I've still got all of this to handle. *Administration.* If I'd wanted to do paperwork, I would've studied harder in school instead of spending my time in the gym."

"Why not bring in someone to manage the business side of the property while Mrs Morgan handles the day-to-day operation?" Graham poured the boiled water into a pot along with a few bags to let the tea sit for a bit. He wondered why BC seemed so set on not being tied down to Cornwall. *Odd.* He thought about it in silence for a few minutes. "Didn't you already settle all of this with her?"

"Yes."

"Then, what's the problem? Don't create shit where it doesn't need to be."

"Lovely visual." BC grimaced at him. He accepted the cup of tea handed to him with a grin. "I've got plans for the coming year that don't include being in Cornwall."

Oh, well, shit.

Awkward.

He wanted to ask if those plans included him. *Too needy? Too soppy?* He decided after cancer his pride didn't matter if his happiness was at risk. "Are you going somewhere?"

"Might be." BC sipped his tea with a complete calm and casualness. Graham wanted to shake him until his head fell off. "Sit, drink your tea, you seem rather stressed."

"Bastard." Graham kicked him in the shin underneath the table. He couldn't bring himself to ask the question. "What about us?"

Or apparently, I can ask it.

Instead of answering right away, BC returned his attention to the chaos on the top of the table. He shuffled through all of the papers, clearly on the hunt for something. Graham could only watch him with a growing weight in his stomach.

Had BC decided all the strain, worry, and fear hadn't been worth it after all? They couldn't be breaking up now, could they? *I am losing my bloody mind.* He tried the breathing exercises Freddie had taught him.

Sodding shit doesn't work.

Breathe in the calm, my arse.

BC finally pulled out a dossier from the bottom of the pile. "Ah, here we go."

"What's this?" Graham caught the folder when it was flung across the table at him. He opened it to find a travel itinerary, along with tickets and maps. "I don't—"

"Want to wander with me?" BC stretched a hand out to

hold one of Graham's. "It can be our New Year's resolution. Show me this wild world you're always going on about in your articles. I want to see it."

"Thought you were afraid of flying?" Graham couldn't look up to meet the man's eyes—too afraid the tears in his own would show. "You were quite vocal about losing your shit on the way to Palau."

"More afraid of losing you." BC released his hand and caught him by the shirt instead to pull him around the table. They kissed desperately with the dossier pressed between them. "Say yes, then. Put me out of my misery."

"Yes. I'd happily wander with you for the rest of my days." Graham struggled to get the words out.

"Of course you would, you're a sentimental numpty."

"Bastard."

"I love you too."

EPILOGUE

Three flights into their world exploration, BC still hadn't quite come to terms with the concept of aeroplanes. He no longer struggled with the urge to vomit—a massive improvement. But having to fly was a sacrifice he would willingly make for the rest of his life if it meant Graham would be happy and healthy.

His wanderer had brightened significantly after their first few trips. Their first journey of the summer months had been to Gansu, China. They'd stood at the foot of the colourful sandstone formations in complete awe of the rainbow-striped mountains.

They would be staying in China for the next few weeks. Becca had helped him with a list of places in the country to check out, ones that Graham had never seen. It had been important to him for this to be a true exploration for both of them.

"Enjoying the roasted pork noodles?" Graham flicked sauce at him. He used the chopsticks with a much greater dexterity than BC had managed thus far. "You could ask for a fork."

"I could." BC scowled at the two slender sticks between his fingers. "I'll master these sodding things eventually."

"Or starve?"

"Or starve."

Stubbornness had gotten him through much of his life. BC couldn't imagine chopsticks would be any different. In the meantime, he used his fingers to toss a chunk of meat into his mouth.

"Sure you don't want a fork?" Graham's green eyes twinkled at him in pure amusement. It was wonderful to see the bright spark back in them. "We should've snuck food in from home for you. You'll starve at this rate."

Ignoring the teasing, BC focused all of his attention on mastering the damned utensils. They'd be in Shanghai for another week. Seven days to learn how to avoid making a complete fool of himself. He could do it, maybe.

The past six months had gone by incredibly quickly. They would spend several weeks traveling at a time, returning to Cornwall for a week for laundry and doctor visits. Freddie and Genevieve had wanted to keep a close eye on their patient to ensure he hadn't begun traveling too soon.

He hadn't.

BC hoped he hadn't.

At times, Graham would lose his patience at the slow pace. It was obvious he wanted to rush through everything. He expected to be climbing up trails, walking the entire Great Wall, not keeping up with the more elderly travellers.

They sat at a table outside the restaurant, enjoying their supper and watching the slowly setting sun. It glinted off the windows of the nearby buildings. The small town shone in jewel tones with none of the choking smog of the larger cities in China to mask it.

"We should get some rest." Graham led the way back to their small hotel room. "We've an early morning tomorrow."

They'd received a few raised eyebrows when they'd insisted on a room to themselves—one without separate beds. It had happened in other countries as well, the ones that didn't have a reputation for being open to the various ways love could manifest itself. BC couldn't help wondering if his height and muscles deterred bigots from taunting them.

Who'd want to tackle a man his size?

Only sodding idiotic bastards.

The concierge at the hotel barely blinked when they jogged up the stairs to their room on the second floor. They'd be checking out in the morning to start their slow journey to Beijing. Their return flight would take off from the international airport in the capital city.

BC could clearly hear sounds from outside through the paper-thin walls of their room. "I almost miss the Fisherman's Refuge—Zeus and all."

"I'm confident the royal pooch doesn't miss you one bit.

Mrs Morgan probably has him sleeping on silk and eating steak from delicate porcelain plates." Graham lifted his head from where he'd been jotting notes in the new travel journal, one Becca had bought as a going away present for him. "It figures my body starts working relatively normally, only for us to be in the one hotel with walls so thin we'd get arrested if we dared to do anything."

BC had been restraining himself all week from acting on the knowledge that Graham's libido had returned to normal. *Well, almost.* He shifted up on the mattress until he was stretched out beside the man. "What's life without a little danger?"

"Not sure I'd call the prisons here a *little* danger."

Fair point.

He hadn't made his mark in rugby by refusing to step up to a challenge. He caught the journal out of Graham's fingers and carefully chucked it onto the open suitcase on the floor nearby. "We'll have to find a way to keep you from shouting my name too loudly."

"Arrogant arse." Graham batted away BC's fingers, which had already started to stray up the inside of his khaki shorts, along his inner thigh. "Quit it. We didn't bring condoms or lube, remember?"

"Shit." BC had always been of the opinion that no matter the rush, one had time for lube. *Always.* "I suppose we'll have to let our fingers do the talking and enjoy the pleasures of everything else when we're safely at home."

Inching his fingers up Graham's inner thigh, BC couldn't help thinking what a relief it was to find it covered in coarse hair. Chemotherapy had taken all of the man's hair; its growth, more than anything, signalled a return to health. He played with them a moment before searching out his prize hidden by a pair of boxers.

He gripped the silken flesh of Graham's cock possessively. *One. Two strokes.* His gaze stayed on the expressive face of the man he loved. He couldn't help smirking at the tight-lipped wanderer, who was clearly struggling to keep from vocalizing his enjoyment at being pleasured.

With his chin resting on the top of Graham's thigh, BC murmured to the man while twisting his fingers up and around his shaft. He slid his free hand into his own shorts. It took a bit of manoeuvring to find the perfect rhythm between them.

In the end, BC had to tilt his mouth down to muffle his own gasps of pleasure, a fact Graham would tease him relentlessly over later, once they'd recovered. As it was, the two men worked hard to explode in perfect silence.

It wouldn't do to shock the neighbours.

"Fuck." Graham dropped a rare F-bomb, sinking down on the bed with a groan. "It feels as if I've waited years to have an orgasm."

BC lifted up a bit to smirk at him. "Want to go for another one? Just to make sure it all works."

Graham whacked him weakly on the side of the head. "Numpty."

"Yeah, yeah." BC found it impossible not to be drawn into those gleaming green eyes. "Love you."

"Oh, don't go all swoony on me because you've come in your pants." Graham grinned tiredly at him. "Might love you as well."

"Of course you do." BC rolled off the bed, wincing when it pulled at his pants. "Time for a wash."

The shower in the bathroom attached to their room was so small BC could barely fit. His head bumped the ceiling whenever he got into it. China hadn't been designed for six-foot-seven former rugby players. He'd hit multiple doorframes, gotten stuck in a seat on the train, and broken more than one chair.

He loomed over everyone, quite literally well over head and shoulders above the crowd. They might've been there to see the sights, but the locals seemed far more interested in the tall British bloke. He'd lost count of the people wanting to take selfies with him.

"Time for the evening comedy show." Graham followed him into the bathroom, perching on the lid of the toilet to watch. "Well? C'mon then."

BC glowered at him. "Numpty."

"Me? I'm not the one trying to contort myself into a shower."

"*Numpty.*"

They giggled. Grown men. Giggled. They did it far more often than others would likely believe.

BC stripped down and squashed himself into the shower stall. "Enjoy the show."

"Dance, dance." Graham dodged the dirty boxers thrown his direction. "Think we'll be this happy in ten years?"

"We'll be too old to remember whether or not we're happy."

"I'm serious."

BC didn't have to lift his head much to look over the top of the sliding doors of the shower to see Graham staring down at his clenched fingers. *Hmm.* "On a scale of one to ten?"

"If you must."

"Definitely a ten." BC had reached the point where he couldn't imagine his life without the ginger wanderer in it. "I'll be even happier if you help me get my back."

"I'm not getting stuck in the shower again. We broke the door last time." Graham snickered, obviously remembering their failed attempt at showering together earlier in the week. "Think they figured out how it happened?"

"Hope not." He couldn't imagine the sweet older man who seemed so completely confused by them being able to grasp what had caused the damage. "Doubt they care as long as we pay for it."

While Graham continued to laugh, BC found himself drawn back to thoughts of whether they'd be happy. Would they? People always said opposites attracted—they were more alike than anything else.

What if his cancer comes back?

BC could imagine far too many what ifs, any of which could derail their life together. He ducked his head under the water to rinse off the shampoo. It terrified him that they might not stay with each other.

Will we be happy?

In ten years?

In twenty?

"You keep thinking so hard, you might break something." Graham reached into the shower to pinch him on the arse. "BC?"

"Yeah?" He tilted his head out of the water to hear better.

"We'll be brilliant, right?"

"Yes. We will." BC grabbed the hand still lingering near his arse to tug the man closer. "Magnificently so."

And they would; even if the cancer came back, they'd be brilliant because they were together.

Brilliant.

THE END

ACKNOWLEDGMENTS

A massive thank you to my betas, Becky, Olivia, and all the brilliant people at Hot Tree, and my beloved hubby who didn't complain too much about all the rugby I was watching (again)—for research purposes, of course.

Thanks to all of my readers, whether this is the first or fourth of my stories that you've read. Hope you love Graham and BC as much as I do.

ABOUT THE AUTHOR

Dahlia Donovan wrote her first romance series after a crazy dream about shifters and damsels in distress. She prefers irreverent humour and unconventional characters.

An autistic and occasional hermit, her life wouldn't be complete without her husband and her massive collection of books and video games.

Stay connected with Dahlia:

FACEBOOK: WWW.FACEBOOK.COM/DAHLIADONOVAN

WEBSITE: WWW.DAHLIADONOVAN.COM

TWITTER: WWW.TWITTER.COM/DAHLIADONOVAN

ABOUT THE PUBLISHER

Hot Tree Publishing opened its doors in 2015 with an aspiration to bring quality fiction to the world of readers. With the initial focus on romance and a wide spread of romance sub-genres, they envision opening up to alternative genres in the near future.

Firmly seated in the industry as a leading editing provider to independent authors and small publishing houses, Hot Tree Publishing is the sister company to Hot Tree Editing, founded in 2012. Having established in-house editing and promotions, plus having a well-respected market presence, Hot Tree Publishing endeavours to be a leader in bringing quality stories to the world of readers.

Interested in discovering more amazing reads brought to you by Hot Tree Publishing or perhaps you're interested in submitting a manuscript and joining the HTPubs family? Either way, head over to the website for information:

WWW.HOTTREEPUBLISHING.COM

www.ingramcontent.com/pod-product-compliance
Lightning Source LLC
Chambersburg PA
CBHW050511190726
48284CB00003B/772